Rebel in Right Field

By the Same Author

THE BIG STRETCH

THE CATCHER FROM DOUBLE-A

FAST MAN ON A PIVOT

GOOD FIELD, NO HIT

HIT AND RUN

LONG BALL TO LEFT FIELD

MISTER SHORTSTOP

SHOWBOAT SOUTHPAW

STARTING PITCHER

SWITCH HITTER

THIRD-BASE ROOKIE

Rebel in Right Field

BY DUANE DECKER

New York, 1961

WILLIAM MORROW & COMPANY

For Johnny McNulty and Faith,
two of the loyal fans in the stands.

Rebel in Right Field

Chapter 1

THE INK WAS HARDLY DRY ON DANNY REDD'S HIGH-
school diploma when he accepted the thousand-dol-
lar check from the world champion Blue Sox. First,
of course, he signed the contract. After that was
over, things happened fast.

They put him in a plane—his first ride in one. A
few hours later, valise in hand, he arrived shortly
before dark to join the Class D Cortland Colonials,
lowliest link in the Sox farm chain. He felt a little
depressed by the dismal look of the rickety, rundown dressing room. But he shrugged. At least it
was pro and you had to start somewhere.

Almost as soon as he had unlocked the valise to
get his glove and spiked shoes, the Colonials' manager came over and introduced himself. Rip Radjecki was the name. When he heard it spoken,

Danny couldn't see in his mind how it might be spelled. It sounded difficult.

Radjecki was as direct and sudden as the ring of a telephone. "You're in right field tonight, Redd," he said. "Also batting lead-off."

"Good," Danny said. "I'm both."

"Both what?"

"A right fielder and a lead-off man."

Radjecki seemed to peer closely at him. He was kind of young for a manager, Danny thought. He had pictured bush-league managers as being old and short and dried-up looking. Radjecki was anything but that. Early thirties. A stern and decisive presence, as though he were in charge of the Blue Sox themselves instead of their seventh-place Class D farm club. His eyes were gun-metal gray, his build was tall and rugged. There was a sort of indestructible look about him. His air of poise and conviction baffled Danny. It didn't fit with his lowly job.

Radjecki said, "I think, Redd, it behooves me to warn you. I'm paid to figure these things out about the sand-lotters turning pro. My job isn't to follow opinions, it's to form them. Let's try to understand each other."

He sounded like a senator or something, Danny thought. His whole picture of pro ball seemed slightly upside down.

"Well," Danny said, sparring for time and feeling flustered, "it's just that I happened to play right field and leadoff all through high school and the Babe Ruth league."

Radjecki let his explanation hang in the air, like smoke from a cigar. What he had said was true. Danny's coaches had all told him he was a natural in both those slots because of his speed, level swing, and skimming line-drive hits.

"I know all about that," Radjecki said finally. "They sent me reports. By the way, something I haven't got a report on—did you play football in high school?"

"No. What's that got to do with it?"

"I just wondered. Basketball?" Radjecki had a swift way of eliminating questions that might untrack him from his train of thought.

"No."

"Just baseball then. How come? Report says you're fast, extremely well co-ordinated. I can see you're reasonably filled out for your age. Didn't the football coach think you had the makings?"

Danny couldn't, for the life of him, see what all this had to do with his playing right field for the Cortland Colonials. But Radjecki had a way of asking questions that pulled you, like a needle to a magnet, into answering with quickness and truth.

"I didn't try out," Danny said. "The football coach asked me to. I said no."

"Why?"

"I don't go for those games where you get banged around," Danny explained. "That blocking and tackling—you can have it. Me, I like baseball."

Radjecki gazed at him thoughtfully. "Those feelings make me wonder what you do, son, when you're chasing an important fly ball and you find a fence in your way?" He had raised the inflection of his voice on the final word so it turned out to be a question.

"I do the best I can," Danny said. "But I don't go crashing into fences like the phony heroes, if that's what you mean."

Radjecki seemed to recoil. He frowned. "Never? You never banged a fence in your life?"

"I've been especially careful of that," Danny said, with pride. "I figure you've got to stay in one piece or you'll never even get a shot at the big money up there."

"Well," Radjecki said mildly, "you've got time enough ahead to straighten out these ideas. That might save you. Because not many ballplayers reach the big show figuring things like a touch-football player."

He strode off as quickly as he had appeared. Danny guessed Rip Radjecki didn't like him much. So what? He was just a Class D manager and Danny didn't figure to stick around Class D very long.

Just then Bartz, the big, husky center fielder of the Colonials, spoke to him. Bartz had the next locker and he had necessarily heard the conversation.

"You shouldn't have talked to Mr. Radjecki that way," Bartz said.

"He asked me what I thought. I told him."

"Don't you know who Radjecki is?" Bartz asked.

Danny puzzled over the question a moment. The name suddenly rang a faint bell. But he couldn't quite place it.

"You must have read about him," Bartz said. "He

was one of the greatest, but he didn't last long. With the Clippers."

Suddenly Danny remembered. He had only been nine or ten years old, but even then he read the *Sporting News*. Sure, it all came back.

"I—I think I do remember," Danny said.

"Just thought you ought to know, so you don't talk to him that way any more."

Bartz turned away. All Danny could do was feel sorry for Radjecki, although he wouldn't have talked to him in such a way if he had remembered. Radjecki's story had been a tragedy. Rookie of the year in his early twenties, league batting champion in his sophomore year—and then his career had ended two years later.

He had been nicknamed the Ripper because he'd challenged fences in every park in which he played, and come off second best so often that he started to spend more time in hospitals than in center field. There had been seven concussions in all, plus broken collarbones and fractured shoulders. He went out as fast as he had come in.

By this time, if he had been careful of himself, chances were he would be making as much money as Mickey Mantle or Willie Mays. Instead, Danny thought, he was probably making four or five thousand a year in Class D.

No doubt he had scrapbooks that could prove his greatness; but the others had money and bowling alleys and restaurants to prove theirs. Danny would take the money, any time. Though he felt admiration for Radjecki, he thought the man had been foolish. No wonder he was so curt. But he must have a lot of patience or he couldn't have listened to the things Danny had said to him and remained so quiet and mild about it. When he saw Radjecki in the dugout later, just before game time, he felt a new respect for the man.

Danny's first game turned out to be a nightmare to him. The lighting system in Colonial Park was so poor that he thought it must take a player weeks to get used to it. He struck out four times in a row. He dropped a fly ball. And he let another one get past him for a triple, because he thought he was about to collide with the two-hundred-pound Bartz in center field. Bartz, it turned out, had changed his course and cut behind Danny, to back him up. If he hadn't done that, the routine fly ball would have been an inside-the-park home run. The Colonials lost the game, 11 to 3.

Radjecki spoke to him at the door of the dressing room. "Look, kid," he said, "I think you need a rest."

If it was meant to be funny, Danny didn't think it was.

"Not," Radjecki added, "because of your whiffs or the muff. Only because of the easy fly you played into a triple, just to protect yourself."

"With my speed," Danny said, "if I'd crashed into Bartz. . . ."

"What good is speed if you don't use it?" Radjecki demanded. "Where do you think your way of playing ball will get you?"

"To the big leagues," Danny said angrily.

"Well, for the present," Radjecki said, "it's got you a quick seat on the bench."

Danny had the idea he wouldn't get much of a chance to play for the Colonials this year.

Chapter 2

THAT HAD HAPPENED THREE YEARS AGO. THINGS, with Danny Redd, were very different now.

He was remembering the incident, that first and only meeting with Rip Radjecki, as he stood in front of the bulletin board in the Blue Sox dressing room at the Blue Sox Stadium. On the board was posted the line-up for this season's opener, due to start in a few hours. The line-up made sweet reading to him. His eyes lingered fondly on it:

Redd   RF
Walker   2B
Woodward   CF
Jaffe   LF
Scalzi   3B
Stookey   1B

Pearson   SS
Gibbs   C
Lasky   P

Smiling a smile of deepest pleasure, Danny went over to his locker, sat down on the bench, and began the ritual of removing his street clothes. Too bad Radjecki couldn't be around right now. He wondered what Radjecki must think, down there in the bush leagues, when he looked over the box scores in tomorrow morning's paper and saw that Danny Redd had made it all the way in three years. Radjecki would remember that he had benched Danny Redd, whom the reporters now called the boy wonder, after one game. The only unsatisfactory part, to Danny, was that Radjecki couldn't know he had made it without trying to bang any fences to the ground.

Radjecki also might not know that Danny Redd had never ridden the bench for a single day with the Cortland Colonials. Because the day after Danny had been benched, the Sox had promoted Radjecki to an emergency job of managing a Class C club; and the new manager of the Colonials had put Danny Redd back into the line-up. He had started to hit in that second game with the Colonials. And he'd never stopped hitting since.

His first season's average had been .304. That had been good enough for him to jump over Class C into B the next year. There the average had bulged to .322. The following year the Sox had taken a long look at him in spring training. In those early exhibition games he had a stretch of nine straight times at bat with no enemy pitcher able to get him out: four singles, two doubles, a home run, and two walks. He finished the Grapefruit League with a .367 average. The sportswriters were booming him as the man ready to move in now and take over in right field for the aging Chip Fiske of the Blue Sox.

The Sox brass had not agreed. They hadn't thought that Danny was ready or that Fiske was through. But last season—that had settled the matter, once and for all.

Fiske slumped to .247; Danny punched the pitching in Triple-A for .331. This year it had been clear from the start of the training season that Danny Redd had arrived, that Fiske would be a bench man.

Danny knew, too, that he represented much more to the Sox than merely a replacement for a worn-out

Fiske. He was a natural-born lead-off man, something the Sox hadn't had since Coach Johnny Madigan had given way at third base to Vic Scalzi. He
had qualifications beyond his ability to hit line-
drive singles in profusion.

He had a good eye for the strike zone. Consequently he could wait a pitcher out, get his share
of the bases on balls. He was a reliable two-strike
hitter. He could bunt with the best of them, and
he had been clocked at 3.3 seconds going down to
first base, clocked at less than ten seconds traveling
the ninety-yard distance from home plate to third
base on a triple. He had stolen twenty-eight bases
in Triple-A. And he socked an occasional line-drive
home run.

There were those who thought he should play
center field because of his speed. But with the
league's All-Star man, Russ Woodward, already
there, it didn't make sense. Besides, right field at
the Stadium was a deep wide pocket and he had a
throwing arm stronger even than Woodward's.

Danny began to put on his clean new creamy-
white uniform, number 22, with the long blue pin
stripe running down each pants leg, the blue sox

with the white rings, the blue cap, the blue sweat shirt. He stood up, a broad-shouldered slim-hipped young man a little under six feet, with a boy's face and a natural grace in every move that he made.

For no good reason at all he thought of a quote his manager in Class B had made to a reporter: "He's the greatest I ever saw at making the running shoetop catch. Usually a ballplayer has to make a dive for them. But not Redd. He keeps coming at top speed, sticks his glove down for the ball, grabs it, and never even breaks stride."

Of course, the manager didn't know it, but Danny had worked on that one to avoid the need of taking a dive. Dives, any bodily contact, he still avoided at every turn. But, so far, his brilliance had somehow concealed the fact.

He felt terribly anxious to get out on the field now, although it was so early many of the players had not yet arrived. He had come early mainly because he felt so nervous. He wanted to get it out of his system and the field seemed the proper place to do that.

Across the big room he saw a tall, rangy man headed toward him. It was Pete Gibbs, the Sox Number One catcher. Pete had the locker next to his own. Danny admired Pete more than he admired anyone else on the team—as solid a man as he was a catcher. To Danny he seemed old, over thirty, but he laughed more than the younger ones, and he made funny cracks in a quiet way now and then. There was something about him that made Danny want to listen when he talked.

He paused in front of Danny, looked him up and down, and said, "Well, Danny, you sure do *look* like a big-leaguer, anyway. Of course, we can't count the votes for a few weeks yet."

"I don't think I feel like a big-leaguer," Danny said. "Not yet."

"What's the matter?"

"I got buttercups in my stomach."

Pete slapped him on the shoulder. "If you didn't have, you'd be the first."

"When does it go away, Pete?"

"Right after you take the first cut at the ball or squeeze that first fly."

Somehow, Danny thought, he believed that what Pete had said was so. Now Pete turned and started to hang his rich-looking navy-blue sports jacket inside the locker. Everything about Pete had a certain air of style and class, even his clothes. That was more than Danny could say for every big-leaguer he'd met.

He heard his name called. He turned quickly and saw Jug Slavin, the Sox manager, standing in the doorway of his small office off at the far end of the big room. Danny walked over rapidly and Jug told him to come in.

Jug sat behind the green metal desk that almost matched the shade of the green carpet and the green walls. He motioned Danny into a chair beside the desk, saying, "I guess you saw the line-up for today's game?"

Danny nodded.

"You've really done something, Danny," he said. "Your name at the top of that line-up in three short years."

"I want to keep it there, Mr. Slavin." In those three years, among other things, he had learned to call a manager Mister until the manager said to call him something else. Nobody was going to call him one of these fresh young rookie punks.

"You've got everything you need to keep it there," Jug Slavin said. "In all the reports I've ever had on you, no manager benched you—except your first one. Guess you remember who I mean?"

The question reminded Danny that he'd always been annoyed at himself for remembering Rip Radjecki so frequently, recalling what the man had said and how he had looked while saying it. Yet he hadn't talked with Radjecki more than a total of maybe ten minutes in his whole life. Why had Radjecki stuck in his mind so sharply and so long?

"Mr. Radjecki was his name," Danny replied. "I know anything *he* said about me wasn't good."

"I think you'd be surprised," Jug Slavin told him. "That's why I dug the brief report he sent me out of the files. Want to hear it?"

Not especially, Danny thought. But he didn't say that, of course. What he did say was, "Sure, Mr. Slavin."

"Well, here goes." Slavin picked a sheet of paper from the top of his desk and began to read:

If you want to get a look at a kid who has all the physical equipment it takes, and then some, check on Danny Redd. I only saw him in practice and in one game and I benched him right after it, but that was strictly in the interest of educating him. He had a bad night, but they all do here, as the lighting system is something you have to get used to, like finding your way through a strange, dark house at night. But this kid, right-handed all the way, showed me a swing that is level, compact, natural—call it his birthright. No one should ever tamper with Redd's swing. Just talk to him about timing, hands, and concentration. He can run like a race horse, he can throw, and he can field. He looks to me as though he might have occasional power, too—maybe a dozen home runs a year. Right now his attitude on some things is wrong, but that may be cleared up by the time he's ready for a look in spring training.

Jug put the paper back on the desk top. "Rip Radjecki, I might add, doesn't fool easily."

Danny was shaking his head as if to clear it. "Mr. —Mr. Radjecki wrote that about *me*?" His voice sounded incredulous.

"Every word. Quote and unquote."

"But I had a terrible night. Struck out four times and. . . ."

"That wouldn't throw Radjecki off. Not if he saw what he saw. And he did or you wouldn't be here."

"It beats me," Danny said. Funny, but he had nursed his grudge inwardly against Radjecki for so long that this high praise from him, coming three years later, left him feeling a little bit foolish. He

had been so sure that Radjecki had thought he'd
never make it.

"Well, I wanted you to hear it before you went
out there for your first big-league game. I want you
to remember what Radjecki said—remember, even if
you do happen to strike out a couple times or muff
a long one, that we can see beyond that, as Radjecki
did. If you can relax, do it. If you can't, well, all
right. It will come. And also remember that there
are the good days and there are the bad days. For
all of us."

Slavin stood up. Danny knew the talk was over.
But it came to him that Slavin couldn't have done a
better job of making him feel unafraid of what he
did out there today. No wonder he had the reputation of being the best manager the Sox had ever
known. And no wonder he held the job year after
year, while other managers were being hired and
fired and rehired and refired up and down the
league.

"Time to get up on the field, Danny."

"I'm ready."

"Strangely, Radjecki never did say what he
thought was wrong with your attitude when you reported to him. He just said that since he'd only

managed you in one game he didn't think it would be fair for him to write an editorial. He simply stuck to the facts as he saw them. Any idea what he meant, Danny?"

Danny thought for a long couple of moments. Why should he bring up that conversation with Radjecki? He'd learned more than baseball in three years. "Can't say that I do, Mr. Slavin. Three years is a pretty long time."

Slavin nodded. His lined, weatherbeaten face broke into a smile. "Yes. At twenty I guess it seems so."

Danny walked out and headed toward the locker to get his glove. Pete Gibbs had already departed. So had almost all the rest. As he strode out of the dressing room, down the spike-chewed steps to the tunnel, he thought, Now how do you figure a guy like Rip Radjecki?

Chapter 3

THERE WAS A PARADE TO THE FLAGPOLE IN CEN-
ter field by the color guard. Then the national an-
them. And of course the mayor threw out the first
ball, which Pete Gibbs bagged. He said it was his
third from the mayor and he always traded them in
with a bookseller he knew whose son was a Sox fan.
"If it keeps up this way," Pete said happily, "I'll
wind up with a library. Who knows?"

The Sox scooted to their positions. As Danny
crossed the infield skin, he heard the rising, joyful
swell of the near capacity crowd in the stands. They
sounded mighty happy that the baseball season was
starting again.

In the right-field bleachers the crowd stood to
roar its welcome. When Danny turned around, the
grandstand was on its feet to express the same ex-

citement. And Danny thought he felt it even more than they did.

He waited and scuffed the grass, feeling tense but ready, while Eddie Lasky threw the warm-up tosses. Lasky was almost forty years old and he was still opening-game pitcher. He couldn't last forever, as everybody knew but Lasky. He no longer had the hop on the fast ball, but he had the craft and the will and the heart. Danny felt buttercups still inside him, but he was no longer afraid of them, after the talk with Jug. Silently he thanked Jug alone, but he knew Radjecki had something to do with it. And he knew he'd remember this moment when he turned sixty.

Kelly, the Clipper lead-off man, stepped into the batter's box. Because Kelly hit left-handed and sometimes pulled the ball, Jug had told Danny to play him fairly deep.

Lasky threw the first one and the crowd screamed, a bullet kind of a scream that pierced the park and probably the city limits. The pitch was wide and Kelly left his bat perfectly still. Then he stepped out, grabbed a little dirt, stepped back in.

Danny thought, With that pitch I'm a big-leaguer. Name in the record books. It's official.

Kelly took low for a second ball. Gibbs walked halfway to the mound and called something to Lasky. Lasky nodded. Gibbs went back and Lasky took the full windup once more. He hit the inside corner and Kelly still did not offer. Gibbs slammed the ball back at Lasky. Lasky touched the resin bag lightly, flicked it away. Then he studied Kelly again and wound up.

This one was a breaking pitch, belt high and in the zone. Kelly lashed. The ball shot on a sinking line, not too high, over second base. Danny saw the ball as he charged, a shiny white streak in the sun. It skimmed over the upflung glove of Bud Walker, the acrobatic Sox second baseman. It was a sinking line drive, the treacherous kind. It was Danny's or nobody's.

Danny had handled these before. He raced. The ball sank even more sharply. Danny gained momentum. He saw that it called for a dive—for most players, that is. Not for him.

Still at top speed he stuck his glove down, like a spade into soft earth. He didn't break stride. His glove was at his shoetops, his patented play. He had done it a hundred times. But never on a ball that sank like this. It was suddenly a golf ball driven off a tee by a duffer, and it simply plopped downward.

He felt the ball hit the glove, but he knew it had hit the turf a fraction of a second before he swallowed it in the pocket. It was so close he couldn't see it touch the turf, but he knew by the lessened impact that it had. Only someone with field glasses could have known the truth. The umpire's thumb was aloft. Danny heaved it, in no special hurry, to Bud Walker at second. Then with deliberate unconcern he turned his back and headed to his position.

The roar of the crowd died as he turned back to the infield. He saw Kelly, jumping up and down almost like a madman in front of the first-base umpire. Kelly was gesturing frantically with his hands to show that the ball had not been caught on the line. The umpire, big and solid as a rock, folded his arms and shook his head—no, no, no.

Manager Shanty Millikin of the Clippers emerged from the dugout and raced to first base as fast as his age, girth, and bowlegs would permit.

The argument was furious and to no avail. Jug Slavin did not even join them, because he knew it was not necessary. It was a decision of judgment; the umpire was wrong but no one actually could know that except Danny Redd.

Danny waited, scuffed grass again, and smiled. He saw the umpire turn his back, saw Kelly and Millikin head for the dugout, shouting back as they retreated.

Danny knew he had been lucky. The ball had called for a dive. But it had worked out. And he heard the voices in the bleachers behind him:

"Oh, you Danny!"

"The greatest, Danny! The greatest!"

"How to rob 'em, kid! How to rob 'em!"

But he hadn't robbed them. The umpire had. It was all the same—Kelly was out.

And if he had taken the dive and caught it cleanly, maybe he'd have a bum collarbone by now. And the ball might have squirted through for three bases.

He had played it right. And the buttercups were gone. Pete Gibbs had called it.

He was on his way.

Chapter 4

As THE INNING DEVELOPED, THE UMPIRE'S WRONG DE-
cision on Kelly's trapped single was important.
Cortez promptly pumped a ground-ball single
through Lasky's legs into center field. Then Marvin
flied meekly to Woodward in short center, but Mansell belted one high off the left-field wall. Jaffe
made a catlike grab of the rebound to hold Cortez
at third and Mansell at second. But the blow would
have scored Kelly. And the situation would have
had *Big Inning* written all over it.

It still did have, as Lasky walked Berry inten-
tionally to load the bases. Skanran, who followed,
was a powerhouse, but so was Berry, and Skanran
hit right-handed. The odds were better. Skanran
shot a long foul into the distant left-field seats, took
two balls, and then fouled out to Pete Gibbs, who

took it leaning into the box seats. What might have been a quick finish for Lasky had turned into just a jittery but scoreless inning. And Lasky was notorious for settling down after a shaky first inning.

Danny was picking his bats from the rack when Jug Slavin walked over to him. "Catch it or trap it?"

"Trapped it."

"I thought we got a break on it. Son, let's get one thing straight: I never ask my players to take any risks in the exhibition games. But they're over. Now we're playing for keeps. Now we give it all we've got."

"I don't know what you mean," Danny said.

"I'll spell it out then. You should have made a dive for that ball. It was the only way."

"I always grab those off my shoetops," Danny said. "I almost never miss."

"You missed this time. Next time, dive."

He turned away. Danny didn't think Jug had a real beef. Kelly was out, because he'd made it look so close. The result was as good as a dive would have been, and maybe better. Diving was for outfielders who didn't have his speed of foot, his sureness with the glove.

He walked toward the plate swinging two bats—

the one he was going to use and the one with the
lead weights in it. He heard the amplifiers blare his
name. The crowd responded with a nice loud
whoop, then hand clapping as he moved to the edge
of the box, discarding the weighted bat behind him.

Whitey Lord, a left-hander, was pitching for the
Clippers today. Lord had pitched nearly as many
opening-day games for them as Lasky had pitched
for the Sox. Both had been bonded twenty-game
winners in their prime and both were still good for
about fifteen in a season. Pete Gibbs had warned
Danny that Lord's fast ball still took off and that he
had a whole fat bag of cute stuff to go with it.

Berry, the league's most talkative catcher, said to
Danny, "You should buy yourself an infielder's
glove, kid. You'll find it handier for scooping up
those ground balls."

"I threw mine away when I quit shortstop,"
Danny said.

"Whadda you mean—quit?" Berry demanded.
"You're still a shortstop!"

"Who knows?" Danny said, laughing at him.

"Not these umpires," Berry said with a baleful
glare at the one behind him.

"The seminar over, Berry?" the umpire inquired.
"It's all right if we get on with the ball game?"

"If I were the commissioner of baseball," Berry
said, "that man in blue at first base would now be
catching a plane to Horner's Corners." Then he
quickly squatted as Danny stepped in.

Danny always planted himself a little nearer the
rear of the box than the front, because he sometimes
made his decision on a ball late. He tapped the center of the plate with his bat to reassure himself that
he had his proper plate coverage. That settled, he
gripped the bat about an inch from the knob and
spread his feet.

He didn't spread them much. It was what he
called a cozy stance, and with most of his weight on
the rear foot it was comfortable for a straightaway
hitter. He had always been one, naturally, from the
sand-lot days. He would meet the ball just where
the pitcher served it. And, unless he was fooled by
the pitch, when his bat met it—certain as the law
of gravity—the inside pitch would skim toward left.
If it came down the middle to him, it would go back
out the middle. If it showed up on the outside, it
would rocket toward right.

Lord threw one that broke over but low, for a ball.

His second one nicked the inside corner for a strike. The third one was poured in, high and hard, but not too high. Danny was in the hole, one and two, and he figured that they figured rookie eagerness would make him go for a questionable one now.

He figured right; they figured wrong. It was close, but just outside. So was the next one, and he still didn't bite. Now he had run the count to three and two, and the Clippers knew why he was batting leadoff.

This time Lord came in with the fast one again and Danny swung. The ball had hit the outside corner of the plate and as a result it ricocheted off the bat, headed for right field on a line, not high enough to escape an infielder's leap. But no infielder had a chance to leap for it. It picked the hole between Skanran at first and Richards at second, stung the turf, and was retrieved by Marvin in right field as Danny made a quick turn at first, then retreated to the bag.

The burst of noise from the stands was sweet music. Skanran held him close to the bag, as all first basemen had been doing since Danny could remember. Bud Walker bunted on the second pitch, not a good bunt, but good enough. With Danny's deerlike run down the path, Lord took a quick look and threw to Skanran to retire Walker.

Russ Woodward stepped in. The switch-hitting center fielder with the movie-actor look was batting right-handed against Lord. He took a ball and a strike and then crashed a long fly ball to left center. Danny tagged up and when the catch was made by Mansell, even his strong arm didn't make Danny slide, going into third. Some ballplayers slid automatically when they moved up on a long fly ball. Not Danny. He could gauge by the distance of the ball whether he could arrive standing up. And always did, if that looked likely.

Now Mike Jaffe was the hitter. The burly clean-up man was nobody Lord chose to fool around with as long as first base was open. Jaffe drew four wide ones and trotted to first as Vic Scalzi strode up from the on-deck circle.

Lord threw a strike and a ball and then one slipped on him. It went into the dirt and Berry couldn't dig it out. When Danny saw it trickling behind Berry, with the stocky catcher chasing it desperately, he knew it could only boil down to a race between Berry and him. And he didn't see how it could be much of a contest.

It wasn't. He sped down the base line, saw Lord rushing in to cover. But he outraced Lord and had crossed the plate standing up by the time Berry threw the ball to Lord.

Scalzi popped up, but as Danny trotted out to right field, he figured he'd had a pretty big inning, all in all, for his first one in the big leagues. He had saved a Clipper score—or scores—in the top half. He had made the only Sox hit and run in the bottom half and, what was more, he had made the run mainly on his own steam, all the way from first.

The crowd gave him a noisy reception in the right-field bleachers, and he tipped his cap. He had an idea he'd be doing a lot of cap tipping out here. There was more than one way to be a hero with the fans. And you didn't have to go around crashing into fences to be one. That's how it had been in the minors; and that was how it would be in the majors.

He could see that already.

Chapter 5

THE SINGLE RUN LOOMED LARGE UNTIL THE SIXTH inning when the Sox went to work on Lord. Again Danny sparked the mild attack.

Lasky had given up five neatly spaced hits that had produced no runs for the Clippers. But Lord was pitching a game that was just as canny, although he had been helped a lot by two fast double plays.

Lasky led off and he struck out. Danny moved in. He had grounded out to third on his previous trip to the plate.

"Hello, shortstop," Berry growled. Danny guessed that was now his permanent name with Berry. It was all right with him—somehow it had the ring of a grudging compliment.

"Just call me Rizzuto for short," Danny told him.

[40]

He looked out at Lord and figured. The first time, Lord was remembering, he hadn't swung at a ball until the sixth pitch; the second time, the fourth pitch. This time Danny decided to gamble that Lord would come in with the first one on the assumption that he would get a free strike. If so, Lord was very much mistaken.

Lord went into his full windup and Danny saw the ball coming right down the pipe, high and hard, but not too high. He came around on it and felt the good wood meet it. It was a line shot over the leaping shortstop's glove, nicely tagged between left and center.

As he made the turn at first he saw Mansell just catching up with the ball. Danny's running style had been likened to that of a road runner, that swift-stepping bird of the Southwest. To a spectator he seemed to be running on his heels. He let his arms hang, instead of pumping them as a track sprinter does. But he had beautiful balance when in motion, almost a glide, as a result of which he could make the turns at the bases without any apparent slow-down.

It was this lack of slowdown going around first that beat Mansell's mighty and accurate throw.

Danny went in sliding, but it wasn't close. Yet the crowd knew that the hit would have been a single for many base runners. As he got up, slapping dust, he heard the huge roar billow out from the stands in front of him and the bleachers behind him.

Walker went for the first pitch, too. He sliced it, on a late swing, into right field. Marvin charged it, but when he saw how far around third Danny was he only faked a throw to the plate, then threw to Kelly standing on second.

Lord acted flustered and walked Woodward. Jaffe hit a towering fly ball to deepest right center, but Mansell was there. Walker ambled easily to third after the catch.

Lord went to three and two on Scalzi, who then fouled off four in a row. Lord gave Scalzi a weary look as he went into his motion once more. This time Scalzi picked the pitch off and slammed it on the ground to third base so hard that it spun Bayer around and he couldn't hold it. Scalzi got a hit on it and the second run of the inning was scored by Walker. Now baseballs began to fly back and forth in the Clipper bull pen at a rapid rate.

Lord walked Stookey to fill the bases. Shanty Millikin went out to the mound to talk with Lord and Berry, who joined them. Millikin decided to stay with Lord and the left-hander justified the faith. Pearson popped to Kelly.

It was still 3 to 0 when Danny batted again, in the next inning. Gibbs led off with a ground-out to Bayer. Lasky flied to right. Danny moved in.

"Hello, Rizzuto," Berry said.

"I'm glad you finally got the name straight," Danny said.

He saw that Bayer, down at third, was playing him fairly deep. That probably meant Bayer had got the word from Berry that Lord would pitch him inside. Bayer hadn't yet learned what a lot of third basemen in the minors had learned: that you couldn't play Danny Redd either deep or shallow, you had to play him medium. He would bunt on depth and slam a sizzler against a man playing him shallow.

He wanted to bunt on the first pitch, before Bayer had a chance to change his position. But the ball was way inside and too high. He waited and watched as Lord nodded at Berry's signal. Bayer hadn't budged. Danny set himself, bat held loosely, but not so that Bayer could see it was held that way.

Lord wound up, kicked, and delivered. The pitch

was coming inside again but low this time. A perfect pitch for a bunt.

Danny's right hand slid up the bat handle, his left hand guided the direction. The ball slid off the bat, hit the ground softly, and as he took off Danny knew it would roll with tantalizing slowness down the line.

Bayer pounced in, picked it up, and whirled to throw. But he didn't throw. Danny was already within one step of the bag. Bayer tossed the ball to Lord.

Skanran, the hulking first baseman, said, "Well, well, if it isn't the fifth infielder."

"You sound more like Berry than Berry does," Danny told him cheerfully.

Now Lord was worried that Danny would steal. Johnny Madigan, in the third-base coach's box, gave him the go-ahead sign if he wanted to go ahead. Lord threw twice to Skanran before he threw to Walker, the batter.

Danny didn't go down. Lord had held him too close. There hadn't been a chance to get a jump on the ball. Danny never figured he was stealing against catchers; always against pitchers. And Lord was a cute one.

Lord threw to first base twice more before the second pitch to Walker and drew jeers from the stands. Walker took a second strike. Now, Danny decided, Lord was giving his full attention to the batter for a change.

He kept his foot on the bag, automatically, until he saw Lord step to his position on the pitching mound. Then he crept off his usual distance—two steps and then the length of his body. He had done it so often he could come to within an inch of what he had been taught was the longest safe lead a runner could take.

Lord, like a lot of left-handers, used identical body movements whether he was going to throw to first or to the plate. But Danny had also learned that a left-handed pitcher couldn't possibly deliver to the plate unless he bent his right knee just a little. Now he saw Lord's knee make that fractional bend; now he knew the throw was going to the plate. He went.

He made the quick pivot on his right foot, then crossed his left foot over his right leg. His body was low as he left, then straightened, as he flew down the line, into its natural running look. He saw Kelly waiting for the ball as he went into the hook slide.

He felt his foot touch the bag, then felt the tag and knew he was safe by the roar of the crowd.

He stood up feeling very good indeed. Lord was rated the toughest pitcher in the league to steal on. And to make the timing perfect, Walker laced the next pitch over Lord's head into center field and Danny came in standing up. He was thinking to himself: three hits, three runs scored. The Sox could see they had a lead-off man by this time.

Woodward flied out to end it. But when Danny went back to right field the fans were giving him another ovation.

In the top of the ninth Lasky looked as though this was one shutout that was not going to get away from him. He faced the meat of the Clipper batting order—Marvin, Mansell, and Berry. Long-ball hitters, every one.

But Marvin looked at a third strike. Mansell grounded to Pearson. Berry looped a soft fly ball to short left that Pearson, Jaffe, and Scalzi converged on, but not one of them could reach it. It had been hit too low to stay up long enough, a cheap hit but a clean one.

That brought Skanran up. He had power to all fields. On the first pitch he exploded a tremendous smash soaring deep to right center. Woodward had been positioned slightly to left center and he was a long way from this ball. So was Danny, but not quite such a long way.

He raced, one eye on the ball as it started to come down. He was catching up to it, traveling at incredible speed, and then suddenly he was aware that he had reached the warning track. He slowed abruptly.

That was all the help Skanran's hoist needed. It went over the bleacher railing—only by a few feet, but over. Danny's final lunge wasn't enough. He knew in the instant the ball disappeared that his quick slowdown at the warning track had made the difference. He knew that he wouldn't have needed to slow down, because he was running, not back into the fence, but diagonally along it.

But the fans were still in a pleasant mood. The Sox were still ahead, 4 to 2, and he had had a good day. The shouts as he returned to position were all good-natured.

"Can't get 'em all, Danny!"

"Gotta learn this field, that's all, Danny boy!"

That was all right. The only thing he didn't like, the thing that looked a little ominous, was the sight of Lasky. He stood on the mound, hands on hips, staring out at Danny. And even from that distance Danny could tell that he didn't look pleased at losing his shutout.

But he struck Bayer out. So he had his win. Those two runs hadn't meant a thing, had they?

Chapter 6

"THOSE TWO RUNS," JUG SLAVIN SAID, "BOTHERED ME even more than they bothered Lasky."

"What's a warning track for?" Danny asked.

"To warn you if you're running into a fence. You weren't running into a fence. You were running almost parallel to it."

"With my speed. . . ." Danny began.

"With your speed it's a shame to have a ball like that go into the seats. Chip Fiske, who's on the bench because of your speed, would have caught that ball. What are you saving your speed for?"

All Danny could think of was what Rip Radjecki had said to him three years ago. Radjecki's voice came back to him now, "What good is speed if you don't use it?"

"I got three hits and scored three runs mainly on my speed, didn't I?"

"You negated it in the ninth."

"What does *that* mean?" Danny demanded.

"It means you made it add up to nothing in my book," Jug said. "You did the same thing in the first inning on Kelly, only you got a break there. I'm starting to wonder if this is what Rip Radjecki meant in his report when he said your attitude on some things was wrong. Is it?"

Jug Slavin was a man to whom it was hard to be untruthful. "I—I guess it was." Danny wished that Rip Radjecki, a man he'd talked to for only ten minutes of his life, didn't always seem to be tangled up in it.

Jug Slavin stared dreamily at the wall. "What a ballplayer he was! Danny, if you hustled the way Rip used to hustle, there's no telling how great you might become."

In his mind Danny didn't buy it. He said, "Mr. Slavin, if Mr. Radjecki hadn't hustled the way you mean, crashing fences, don't you think he would have lasted up here for maybe fifteen years instead of four?"

"Son, if he hadn't hustled that way he never

would have made it at all. End of conversation. I wanted you to know what was in my mind after this first game. You can act accordingly. And, Danny, you were a marvel on those base paths."

Danny left. The dressing room was almost deserted now. Jug had waited until after he had showered and dressed before calling him into the office. He saw Pickles, the clubhouse man, talking with Chip Fiske as they drank Cokes by the cooler. They nodded, but said nothing as he walked by. He knew Fiske resented him, but any veteran had a right to resent a rookie who took over his job. He probably would himself, in time. But there was no question in his mind that he had taken it over now.

He went to his locker to get his sports jacket. It had seemed like a fine one to him, down on the Rapid City Blues, but it didn't seem so any more. Too gaudy. He was going to get a dark, rich-looking one like the one Pete Gibbs wore.

He headed out the players' entrance and exit and decided to splurge on a taxi to the hotel. He didn't know the city, and he was temporarily a loner because his roommate, a rookie pitcher, had been sent back to Rapid City for another season.

As he started to go through the parking lot, sur-

rounded by high wire screening, where the Sox
players who drove to home games kept their cars,
he heard his name called. He went over.

Pete Gibbs sat behind the wheel of his black
Jaguar and motioned him to get in. Pete was married, but he lived on the west coast and never got
a chance to go home during the season. Sometimes,
he said, his wife and two boys joined him when the
Sox were on a western swing. He always said he
looked forward to the day when the Sox gave him
the boot and he had to go to work, but nobody believed him. And nobody worked harder than Pete,
once the season started.

"I was waiting for you," Pete said. "Hop in,
roomie."

"Roomie?"

"For a fact," Pete said. "You lost yours and I lost
mine and our traveling secretary put us together."

"That's great!" Danny said.

"I think so too," Pete told him.

And then suddenly Danny remembered that Pete
Gibbs had the reputation of being the man the Sox
always placed as roommate to a rookie who looked
like a problem.

"Swell coincidence," Danny said. "If it is a coincidence."

Pete didn't reply to that. "Jug and you had a session?"

"He had the session. I didn't."

"Not good?"

"It was about Skanran's home run. He thinks I should have caught it."

"Well, that was obvious," Pete said. "So now you won't make a mistake like that again. After all, it was your first game. And you played a real game out there, Danny."

He swung the handsome car out of the lot and moved into the downtown traffic. They rode in silence for a while. Danny enjoyed the heavy city traffic and the way Pete snaked his car through it. You could tell he knew this route like the back of his hand.

After a while he said, "Too bad about old Fido Murphy."

"What about him?" Danny asked. Fido had been a coach for the Sox for years.

"He had to call it quits," Pete said. "Doctor's orders. That's why he wasn't around today. First opener he's missed in probably twenty-five years."

"Who's the new coach?"

"Nobody yet, so far as I've heard."

At the hotel, Pete turned the car over to a garage attendant. This was really living it up, Danny thought. Some day he'd have his own car in town. And, he decided, it would be a Jaguar.

They ate together in the hotel dining room and each signed his check, for the club to pay. Nothing like the big leagues, Danny thought. He never wanted to leave them. He had eaten steak, rare, with French fries. He could eat that every night from now until he was eligible for the pension plan. Pete had eaten lamb stew. Pete was an odd one in some ways.

In the lobby, Pete said, "Well, what do you think, Danny?"

"Me for a movie," Danny said.

"Count me out," Pete said. "I'm in the middle of a book I want to finish."

"What's it about?" Danny asked.

"Africa," Pete said, and headed toward the elevator. Danny looked after him, shaking his head in wonderment. Imagine the All-Star catcher being soft for books about Africa! Pete never stopped surprising him. He was lucky to have a roommate like Pete.

He went over to the newspaper counter to get one and see what the movie line-up was. As he approached it, a man who had just bought a paper turned around and they almost collided. Danny stared in utter amazement, his mouth open though he was speechless. The man thrust his hand out.

"Danny Redd!" he said. "You've filled out some, son."

"How—how are you, Mr. Radjecki?" Danny asked.

"Fine. Just fine. Eaten?"

Danny nodded.

"I haven't. My plane was late. Guess I'll put on the feed bag. See you tomorrow."

"Tomorrow?" Danny said. He knew he was sounding all mixed up, but that was how he felt.

"At the Stadium," Radjecki said.

"But I thought you were managing one of the farm clubs."

"I was supposed to again this year," he said. "But it was all changed, now that Fido Murphy retired."

"You mean you're the new. . . ."

Radjecki nodded happily. "The new coach, yes.

It's sure great to be back in the big leagues. See you, Danny."

He turned and strode off. Danny stared after him. This didn't come under the heading of what he called good news. He didn't feel like seeing a movie any more. He headed toward the elevator and went up to the room.

Chapter 7

DANNY FELT A SENSE OF AMAZEMENT AT WHAT HAP-
pened when Rip Radjecki made his official appear-
ance as a Sox coach. It was almost as though
someone from baseball's Hall of Fame had appeared
in person. And yet, behind Radjecki, there had been
only two really good years of big-league play. How,
he found himself asking himself for the second time
in two days, do you figure a guy like Radjecki?

Every player on the Sox, singly or in groups, went
over to his locker to shake his hand, tell him how
glad they were that he was with them. The younger
ones introduced themselves and told him how much
they'd heard and read of him in his playing days.
The Babe himself couldn't have caused a more spon-
taneous show of affection, respect, and even awe.

Radjecki's still-young face showed his deep pleasure. Yet there was a modesty about the man that showed through the pleasure.

After a while Jug came out of his office and called them into a circle while he made one of his rare speeches. It was all about Radjecki, of course, and how grateful Jug felt that after losing such an able coach as Fido Murphy they could find such a fine replacement as Rip Radjecki. He said that Radjecki typified the spirit in teams that won pennants, and that he was sure some of Radjecki's championship fire would rub off on many of them. Danny had the idea Jug's glance paused on him as he made that closing remark.

The same thing happened all over again when they trooped up on the field. All the Clippers, man by man, seemed to find the time to go over near the Sox dugout to shake hands with Radjecki. They were all sorry he was with the Sox, instead of with the club for whom he'd played.

Danny happened to be near, at the bat rack, when Shanty Millikin, the Clipper manager, came over. He heard Radjecki say with a smile, "The Clippers were my only club, but now I'm with the Sox and I'm going to do everything I can to help beat your brains out."

Millikin started to laugh. "You don't think that's a statement with any news value, do you, Ripper?"

Along with the Clippers, the reporters and the TV and radio broadcasters took turns surrounding him. You might have thought it was Eisenhower returning to Normandy or something, Danny decided.

But the prize stunt of all, to him, was when the voice from the amplifiers—after going down the Sox line-up—suddenly boomed, "Returning to the big leagues today, and coaching on first base for the Blue Sox—Rip Radjecki!"

That announcement was followed by a two-minute standing ovation from the crowd as the Sox trotted to position and Radjecki was forced out of the dugout by Jug Slavin to give a quick tug to the visor of his cap as he looked around at the crowd. Announcing a coach over the public-address system was something Danny had never heard before and he doubted that he would ever hear it again.

Sam Sloat, once called the Showboat Southpaw, was the Sox pitcher today. He had come up to the Sox with what had been labeled the fastest fast ball since Feller. A ligament tear had taken that speed from him abruptly. But he had made good with fine

control, an exceptionally sharp curve, and an assort-
ment of other pitches. Though he was young—not
much older than Danny—he pitched the kind of
crafty game that only veterans usually knew how to
pitch. He was noted for being especially tough
with men on bases.

Sloat found himself in a jam in the first inning,
though it was not a jam of his own making. Millikin
was a manager who constantly switched his batting
order. Today, with a left-hander going for the Sox,
he switched Kelly from the lead-off spot to eighth,
and Richards from eighth to lead-off. Richards led
off with a puny pop-up that just managed to fall
beyond the reach of the lunging Scalzi. It kicked
chalk on the foul line and twisted toward the seats.
Richards wound up on second base with the sickliest
double of the season.

Sloat, on a three-and-two count, fooled Cortez
completely with a slider across the knees. Then
Marvin smashed a streak of a ground ball off
Walker's shoulder, which the official scorer called
an infield hit. There were men on first and third
now with one out. The blaster, Mansell, was up.

Sloat threw him a slow curve that hit the inside
corner of the plate for a strike. Then Mansell up-

percut the second pitch and it rode deep, but foul, in the distant left-field corner. Sloat threw him a waste pitch for ball one. Mansell fell away from a high inside curve for ball two. Mansell started to swing on the next one, then checked it. This was a side-arm humpbacked curve that looked like a sand-lot lob, but it touched the outside edge of the plate for strike three. Mansell argued furiously. Shanty Millikin came out of the dugout to join him. Naturally it changed nothing.

That left it up to Skanran, who had been moved to fifth in the batting order while Berry was dropped to sixth. Skanran went for Sloat's first delivery, a curve that broke sharply. His fly was deep to straightaway center, but high, and Woodward was there in plenty of time to take it in. The crowd gave Sloat a nice hand as the Sox went in to bat.

Coots was pitching for the Clippers today. Pete Gibbs said there was some magic connected with Coots. He'd had a 17 and 7 record last year with an earned-run average of 5.4. It just seemed that, when Coots pitched, the Clippers climbed all over the man pitching against him. Pete's opinion of Coots was not a very high one.

Coots could throw hard. Danny saw that on the

first pitch, from which he fell away. Ball one. Then
Coots curved one across the letters which Danny
took for a strike. He took a second strike, which
angered him because he thought it was low. He
turned and told the umpire so. The umpire did not
deign to reply to a raw rookie. But Berry did.

"Kid," he said, "after this next one you can go
back to the dugout and have a good cry for yourself.
I'll lend you my towel."

Danny was too busy watching Coots to reply.
That was the whole purpose of talkative catchers
anyway—to distract you before the next pitch, so
that you were not bearing down in the concentration department. He concentrated on Coots.

Coots threw one that was away from him, but it
was too close to the strike zone to ignore, with a two-
strike count. Danny pushed his bat out at it with a
sort of protective half-swing. He was hoping for a
foul. But the ball bounced high in fair territory,
bounced again and again. Richards had the only
play. But the bounces beat him. Danny made the
bag for an infield hit by a full step. The crowd gave
him a happy yell. Radjecki, in the coach's box,
cupped his hands and called, "Nobody can throw
out a rabbit, Danny! Nobody!"

Walker bunted on the second pitch. The pulled-in infield didn't have a play at second. Walker was out at first.

Woodward drove a line drive that was a shot, but right at Richards. Richards threw to Kelly on second, but Danny scrambled back in time.

Then he had his first look at Mike Jaffe doing what he was paid that big salary to do. With three balls and no strikes on him he swung on a fast ball that wasn't quite fast enough to get by the huge clean-up man.

The long ball to left field was Jaffe's specialty and this was one of them. Danny did not think he had ever seen a baseball hit harder. It wasn't just the length of the trajectory that astounded him—it was the soaring height as well. There was no question, from the moment the ball left his bat, that it was far, far out of the park.

It cleared the wall in left with yards to spare and disappeared somewhere in the railroad tracks beyond. Danny watched it all the way, knowing he didn't have to hurry as he rounded third and looked back over his shoulder. He waited at the plate to shake Jaffe's hand, along with the next hitter, Scalzi, and Archie, the bat boy.

"What kind of a ball did you hit?" Danny asked him.

Jaffe grinned. "One I liked, that's all I know."

Danny decided that he'd like to find out how it felt to hit a big-league home run. He hadn't tried to pull a ball yet. It seemed about time.

Chapter 8

Tʀᴜᴇ ᴛᴏ ꜰᴏʀᴍ, ᴛʜᴇ Cʟɪᴘᴘᴇʀs sᴛᴀʀᴛᴇᴅ ᴛᴏ ɢᴇᴛ sᴏᴍᴇ runs for Coots. They started in the second inning when Berry led off by belting a line-drive single over first, just out of Stretch Stookey's reach as he leaped. It gunned its way down the right-field line. But Danny had been playing Berry to pull, as advised, and he made a nice stab of it in the corner. His quick, hard throw to second gave Berry pause as he rounded the bag. He went back.

Bayer then pulled a neat one. With a two-run deficit the Sox didn't figure Bayer to bunt. The infield moved in a little, but not much. With a ball and a strike on Bayer, the Sox shortstop, Andy Pearson, broke toward his left as he sensed that the hit-and-run was on. It was on, quite definitely, as Berry raced toward second. But Bayer very neatly

splashed a ground ball through the very spot that
Pearson had just vacated. It would have been a
double play if he had not moved. But the move had
been technically right, because Berry had made the
break to second and Pearson had been instantane-
ously on the alert. The trouble was, Bayer had been
equally alert. And had struck with the precision of
a pool player.

Now Sloat had another jam on his hands. Kelly
bunted both runners along, leaving a situation of
men on second and third with one out, and the
pitcher, Coots, coming up.

Coots was not a good hitter. You could tell that
just by looking at his stance at the plate. He
watched one strike go by, then swung in futile
fashion at a second. He took a ball. And then the
fourth pitch got away from Sloat. It looked to
Danny as though he had meant it to be a screwball,
one of the many freakish pitches Sloat had mastered
after losing his fast ball. But it had too much of the
turn of the screw on it and it nicked Coots in the leg.
That loaded the bases with one out, Richards coming up.

There was a brief conference among Sloat, Pete

Gibbs, Vic Scalzi, and Stretch Stookey. Then they all returned to position and Sloat faced Richards.

Richards was in no rush to offer. He probably had the idea that Sloat might be a little bit upset by having lost Coots with two strikes on him. He managed to run the count to three and two, and then he caught a fat one and slammed it deep to right center.

It was right down the very slot that Danny could remember even after three years. It was right where the ball had been hit in his first game with the Cortland Colonials, the one that had gone for a triple, because he'd thought he was about to collide with Bartz. Bush league or big league, identical balls were hit day in and day out. The ones that turned out well you remembered almost forever and treasured; the bad ones came back to haunt you. This one of Richards had come back to haunt him.

He felt the pistonlike pump of his legs, knew he'd reached the top of his speed. He heard the onrushing Woodward, neither sure which could reach it, if either could. It was that maddening thing—a perfectly placed drive. He felt the moment come when he had to make the decision. He took his eye off the ball for a quick glance toward Woodward at the same moment that he heard Woodward yell, "Take it! Take it!"

It was too late. If he hadn't taken his eye off the ball he might have reached it. But he had and he had slowed down in the process. Now there was no chance. He knew that, even after his final desperate lunge fell short and the ball skidded on to the fence, Woodward after it.

It was a triple that cleaned the bases and the Clippers were out in front, 3 to 2. He saw Sloat looking out at him and scratching his head, cap lifted. Woodward was looking at him, too. Then he stopped looking, turned his back, and returned to position. Behind him he heard his first big-league boo.

"Shouldda had it, Redd! Shouldda had it!"

Annoyed, Danny returned to position. Sloat struck out Cortez, but Marvin singled to center and the fourth run came in. Mansell grounded out. The Coots' magic still held.

As Danny trotted in to the dugout, Rip Radjecki passed him, heading toward the coaching box. Radjecki stared at him in something that looked like wonderment.

"For a minute there," Radjecki said, "I thought it was you and Bartz back together again."

"Thanks," Danny said angrily.

"I could partly excuse it down there," Radjecki said. "But now you're up where there are no excuses. Time's run out that way."

"Thanks again," Danny said, and went on to the dugout.

Woodward came over to him. "Didn't you hear me tell you to take it?" he asked.

"I heard you," Danny said, "but it was too late."

"Well, after this," Woodward said, "you keep running until you hear me yell. Don't stop to take a look at where I am. Have we got that straight?"

Danny nodded and Woodward walked down to the other end of the bench.

Jug Slavin walked over as Danny was rinsing his mouth at the water cooler. Slavin said, "Radjecki told me he saw you do that very same thing in the only other game he ever saw you play. Is that right, Danny?"

"That's right," Danny said.

"Well, you're honest, and I like that," Jug said, as he turned away.

Danny was suddenly full of a fierce sort of anger.

He tried to tell himself he was angry at Woodward for not calling sooner, at Radjecki because he'd reminded him of that first rookie game, and at Jug Slavin for having listened to Radjecki. But he knew he was really only angry with one person. Himself.

Pearson led off the Sox half of the inning by fouling out. Pete Gibbs crashed a ball off the wall in left center on which he made a double. Danny knew that *he* would have had three bases on it. Sam Sloat popped up and then Danny moved in, determined to pull a ball for the first time in the Stadium.

Berry chortled at him. "Thanks for all those nice runs, old buddy," he said.

Again Danny refused to reply. He fixed his eyes on the man at the mound. Berry still wouldn't quit.

"At that," he said, "you might have injured yourself in some disastrous way if you had not used the old noodle. That's what I like to see, a ballplayer using his noodle. Just so long as he is not on our side."

"Enough chatter, Berry," the umpire said. "Let's play a little baseball."

"Suits me fine," Berry said, and he chortled again.

Danny remembered that an angry ballplayer is a bad ballplayer. He watched Coots and tried to decide if he would come in with his fast ball. He didn't. Danny took it, outside, for a ball. He took a second ball, then glanced down the third-base line at Johnny Madigan for the sign. Madigan told him to swing away.

Coots came in with the fast ball this time. Danny had anticipated it. He came around, felt the solid smash, and saw the rising line of the ball as he sped toward first. Before he reached first he knew his shot was going to clear that left-field wall. Not by yards, like Jaffe's, but by enough inches. He slowed to a trot on the way to second.

The cry from the crowd told him that they had expected no such blast from him. They had been content with his singles and his speed. This was pure bonus.

Gibbs, waiting at the plate to shake his hand, said, "A sweet blow, Danny. Just plain sweet."

"Well, now they know I can get right down on the end of the handle, anyway," Danny said.

That tied it up at 4-4. It became a seesaw with both pitchers in constant trouble but never giving up the big inning that would have settled matters. The Clippers picked up a run in the fifth, the Sox tied it in the sixth. The Clippers got two more in the seventh, the Sox got one in the seventh and pushed two more across in the eighth. When the Clippers came to bat for the last time, they were trailing 8 to 7.

Richards flied out, but Cortez singled. Marvin was safe on an error by Pearson, putting men on first and second. Mansell flied harmlessly to left, and Sloat was only one out away from a badly pitched victory. But then he walked Skanran to load the bases, and Jug Slavin was out of the dugout, motioning with his left fist aloft to the bull pen. Phil Doyle, who was both a spot starter and a relief man, came in.

Danny stood with hands on hips, waiting. Suddenly he was aware of Jug motioning toward the dugout. And, with a sense of almost incredible shock, Danny saw Chip Fiske coming out of the dugout, headed toward right field on the trot.

The crowd let out a roar. Fiske reached him and said, "The Skipper sent me to play this last out."

Danny knew, of course, that Fiske couldn't be kidding. Nobody kidded about a matter like this. He felt too choked up to reply. He turned and trotted in, hearing the ovation the right-field stands were giving their old favorite, Fiske.

At the dugout, nobody said anything to him, not even Jug. Danny walked over to the entrance to the tunnel and stood there. Phil Doyle finished the warm-up tosses, then faced Berry.

It took just one pitch. Berry swung at Doyle's first one. It shot on the ground to Walker, who picked it up, zipped to Stookey, and the ball game was over.

It was over, Danny thought as he headed down the tunnel to the clubhouse steps, just one pitch too late.

Chapter 9

HE WAS FURIOUS, AND HE WAS TELLING PETE GIBBS just how furious he was. They were in their room at the hotel that night. He hadn't even had any appetite for steak. He'd left half of it on his plate.

"In two games," he was saying, "I break in with five out of eight, including a two-run homer. And they yank me!"

"For last-minute defensive purposes," Pete said. "It's done all the time."

"On the last out?" he demanded. "With bases loaded? How did it make me look in the eyes of those fans?"

"Danny," Pete said, "try to calm down. It made sense. If I'd been Jug I think I would have done the same."

"But *why?*"

"You know why. You tell me."

"Because of Richards' triple?"

"Yes. That and other things that happened in right field yesterday. It was clear you don't go all out, Danny. You protect yourself instead of the team."

"I play ball the way I played ball for three years and that way got me up here. But fast."

"Well, you're a fast man, Danny." Pete leaned toward him. "Tell me, what got you started playing ball this way? I mean, afraid of getting hurt."

"You think I'm afraid to get hurt?"

"That's obvious."

"Radjecki said that," Danny replied angrily.

"We all have seen it, kid. In two games we all have seen it and we don't want it to go on. I ask again. Why did you start playing ball this way?"

Danny knew where it had all started, but he never liked to think about it. Now Pete was making him remember Big Doug. Big Doug Redd, his brother. Doug had been twice the ballplayer Danny was. He'd been larger, stronger, older. He could hit balls the way Mike Jaffe hit them. That is—Doug could hit them that way sometimes.

Danny had just started high school when Doug

had finished. Doug had played semi-pro for a year. Then he had been signed by a nearby professional team, Class D. He had moved up to C and to B and to A. But all along the line, just when he was having the kind of season he was sure would attract a big-league scout, he hurt himself. It wasn't lack of ability that had stopped Big Doug from rising above Class A. It was his habit, like Rip Radjecki's, of always hurting himself: crashing a fence, or crashing a catcher coming home on a close one, or crashing the second baseman to take him out on a double-play ball.

The net result had been that Big Doug had come home after five years of baseball—four pro and one semi-pro—with no hope of going on, knowing nothing about making a living any other way. He had worked on construction jobs for a while, started to drink heavily, finally been drafted by the Army. Danny still believed Doug could have made it all the way if he had only taken care of himself. He didn't like to think about the defeated lost look of Big Doug when he had finally quit baseball after his release.

He tried now to tell this to Pete Gibbs. Pete listened and never once interrupted. When he finished, Pete said, "I can imagine after that, finding your first manager was Rip Radjecki who had it all cut short, too—well, I can imagine how you felt."

"I'm glad you can imagine it," Danny said.

"But you've got to get over it," Pete said, "or you won't last as long as Radjecki or your brother."

They stopped talking about it after that.

The next day, the final game of the Clipper series, a right-handed pitcher named Dittmer started to warm up for them. Jug hadn't posted the line-up on the bulletin board today, since Millikin's selection for the third game was still unknown. Once it was known, Jug wrote it out in the dugout, and stuck it on the wall with Scotch tape. Danny looked at it and saw that Walker was leading off, Fiske was batting second and playing right field.

After a while Jug called Danny over and asked him to sit down beside him in the far corner of the dugout. "You have seen the line-up for today's game, of course," Jug said.

"Yes."

"For the present," Jug said, "I'm going to do something I've avoided in recent years—platooning. Against right-handed pitching, Fiske is out there. Against left-handed pitching, you are out there."

Danny thought about it. Chances were that they would face three right-handers, at least, for every left-hander. It wasn't just that there were more right-handers around; it was also a fact that the Sox batting order was dominated by right-handed power. That meant he'd play one out of three games, at best.

He said, "I hit right-handers as well as left-handers. I always have."

"So I've heard. It's not chiefly for that reason, the hitting, that I've decided to platoon. It's that you don't seem to be quite ready for the big leagues in your defensive play. I want to give you a chance to see how Fiske plays that field out there."

"All right then," Danny said.

"But don't waste a minute of your time on the bench. You can study and learn a lot, Danny."

Danny stood up. "This is the first game I ever missed since I've been playing pro ball."

"It may do you some good," Jug said.

Danny doubted it. He noticed that most of the team let Chip Fiske know, one way or the other, that they were glad he was back in the line-up.

"Old Fishnet Fiske!" he heard Lasky say to him. "Can't turn him out to pasture."

"No sirree," said Willie (the Lion) Simms, the bull-pen catcher, "not a man can spook fly balls like that little old shrimp."

Danny watched Fiske closely in batting practice—he'd never bothered before. He had been too sure that Fiske was out of the picture, except as a pinch hitter, or fill-in for an injury. He knew, by reputation, that Fiske had been a great second-spot batter with his ability to hit behind the runner, his knack for spraying hits to all fields. In batting practice, faced with easy lobs, he demonstrated just how well he could still do it. But he didn't look quick, and Danny knew how Fiske's batting average had sagged last year.

Joe Rodriguez was the Sox pitcher today. Rodriguez, whose losing battle with the English language down through the years made him a reporter's delight, was a steady, though unspectacular, pitcher. He always won more than he lost, though he'd never had a twenty-game year yet.

He seemed to be in good shape today. He set the Clippers down in order over the first three innings. Meanwhile, the Sox threatened in the second, but failed. They threatened again in the third and this time it was left up to Fiske. Men on first and third, two outs. Fiske had fouled out in the first inning.

Now he waited in his tight, strung-wire stance, bat choked slightly as Dittmer delivered. He took a strike and reached down for some dirt to rub on his hands. He took two balls and then he topped a weak roller that trickled between the mound and third. Bayer raced in and scooped it with a bare-handed grab. The Fiske of other years, Danny felt sure, could have beaten this one out. But no more.

The ball reached Skanran's mitt just before Fiske's foot came down on the bag. And then he crashed, hard, into Skanran. Skanran was about six feet, four inches, and no doubt weighed somewhat over two hundred pounds. Fiske looked about half his height and weight, though of course he was bigger than that. But it was a David crashing a Goliath, and Fiske crashed so hard the ball was jolted loose from Skanran's glove.

Fiske went down in a heap and Skanran turned on the umpire with a roar. The umpire had jerked his thumb upward, then switched to palms spread down. Richards came over from second, Berry came up from the plate, Dittmer from the mound. All four argued so long the umpire pulled his watch after a while. They returned to positions, still growling. The official scorer gave Skanran an error. The Sox had a run in, with Walker on second and Fiske on first. Fiske had a wide grin on his face and Skanran a deep scowl.

Danny knew that Fiske had rammed that run in by crashing into Skanran. Nobody could prove it. And the veteran didn't even act shaken up from his collision with Skanran, the walking mountain. All around him Danny heard the buzz of Sox voices, excited over the way Fiske had managed to butt that run in. All Danny could think was, if Fiske hadn't slowed down so much he could have beaten that one out with no football plays.

Woodward flied out and that inning was the last one in which the Sox damaged Dittmer. Rodriguez, in constant trouble from then on, always managed to slip out of the trap. The goose eggs were strung out. The Blue Sox couldn't seem to buy a hit after that third inning. And when Rodriguez turned the Clippers back in the top of the ninth for a clean sweep of the opening series, it wasn't Rodriguez' back that they pounded as much as it was Chip Fiske's when he trotted in.

Danny thought about it, under the shower. Fiske

had failed to get a hit in five times up; he had only made a couple of routine plays in the field. And yet, no question about it, he had won that game by crashing into the huge Skanran on what seemed like a fairly unimportant play in the third inning.

Then Danny reminded himself of what he considered to be a very important fact—that he, Danny Redd, wouldn't have needed to crash into Skanran. He would have beaten the throw by a full step and maybe two.

Chapter 10

THE SOX MOVED FROM THE STADIUM TO HELP THE Chiefs open their season. By one of those odd quirks, while the Sox had won their first three, the Chiefs had lost all of theirs. This, however, didn't make the Chiefs a soft touch. If anything it made them rough in the eyes of the team. The law of averages said the Chiefs would pick themselves off the floor, because they had power even if they didn't have much pitching.

Since it was a short hop—there would be no western swing until the following week—the team moved by train instead of plane. It was the train trip that made Danny realize, suddenly, that he was a loner except for Pete Gibbs. Everyone else was polite but aloof. He knew they thought he didn't yet belong and he had a pretty good idea why.

It was nice to ride Pullman and have a special car just for the team. He still remembered those bumpy bus rides with the Colonials and others. Pete Gibbs got mixed up in a game of bridge when the train pulled out, so he found himself alone with a newspaper for company. He didn't feel much like reading and just stared out the window at the gentle, sloping hills so richly green this early in the spring. He listened to the rhythmic, unceasing sound of the train and thought again about his brother, Big Doug.

Big Doug, like Rip Radjecki, had used himself up before he'd had a chance for all the big things. Things that would have come in the prime—which to a ballplayer was usually the middle and late twenties. He remembered reading about Pistol Pete Reiser and how the same thing had happened to him and his wonderful talent. He thought of Big Doug now, a PFC in the Army and determined to make the Army his career, because he didn't have a career any more. He knew he was brooding and ought to stop it.

He opened the paper, automatically, to the sports section.

The heading on a column caught his eye. It was by Bernie Glaser, an ex-big-league pitcher turned sportswriter. Glaser's column, he knew, carried a lot of weight with the Blue Sox fans. The heading and the article said:

New Chip off the Old Block

After yesterday's game which Our Side won when that aged, tired cripple named Chip Fiske went for the downs right through the Clippers' resident giant on first base, we are no longer sure of who's in right for the Sox this season. After the game, club trainer Jake Brennan insisted that Fiske be given a look by club doctor John Dougherty. Doc Dougherty took the look and reported his verdict with an ill-concealed smile of satisfaction. Chip Fiske is still a rubber ball when it comes to bouncing off the big fellows and the fences. He had a little bruise on his shoulder and that's all. It was no surprise to me. Down through the years he's absorbed so much punishment that I think he's safely beyond possibility of destruction.

That's good news to Sox fans. Fiske may be well past his prime but what a good man he is to have on any club's bench! We've got a whiz in Danny Redd, but he hasn't caught the big-league fever yet and he may still be a year away. He can do everything a ballplayer is supposed to do except just that one vital thing—risk himself instead of risking the loss of the ball game. It's a pity. . . .

Danny put the paper down as he heard somebody speaking to him. He looked up. It was Rip Radjecki, passing through.

"This is better than those Cortland buses, eh Danny?"

"Sure is, Mr. Radjecki."

"I don't go for that Mister stuff much," he said. "Rip suits me fine."

He sat down in the next chair, which was empty. Danny knew Radjecki was being friendly, and he could use some friendliness. At the same time he knew he was not Radjecki's kind of a ballplayer and for that reason he felt uncomfortable with the new coach.

"I don't expect you to believe this," Radjecki said, "but I honestly thought you were the best man I had on that Cortland team—for the future, I mean."

"I heard you gave me a good report," Danny said. "I was surprised. It convinced me you were fair. But if you think you can talk me out of believing what I believe. . . ."

"Not for one minute would I try," Radjecki cut in. "That's something you'll have to figure out for yourself. Nobody can do it for you." He arose. "It was the same with me. Nobody could have changed my rookie ideas either. And if I had it to do all over again I'd do it the same way. See you, Danny."

The Chiefs had a bad day for their opener. A mist hung over the field and though the rain which threatened never came, it managed to keep the crowd down and the outfield grass wet.

Jug Slavin went with Phil Doyle, who had a good record against the Chiefs. They went with Bracken O'Neill, a right-handed curve baller, so Fiske started in right field.

Walker led off with a smart single through the hole between short and third. Fiske tried to cross them up with a slap into left field instead of the bunt they expected. But, among other things, Fiske's timing on a delayed swing wasn't what it used to be. Killiber at third leaped and grabbed the soft pop and fired to first, doubling Walker. When Fiske returned to the dugout, he sat down and rested his chin on his fists and looked as though if he so much as opened his mouth a growl instead of words would come out.

Woodward, batting left-handed against O'Neill, laced a line drive shot down the right-field line and went into second with a standing-up double. Jaffe walked. Scalzi beat out a high bounder. Danny was thinking what a big inning this would be now except for Fiske's double-play pop. Glancing down the dugout line at Fiske, he guessed the veteran was thinking just about the same thing.

Stookey stepped in. Stookey was a left-hander all the way. He was built trimly, like a light heavy-weight boxer, and his RBI score was always a lot more impressive than his batting average. He took two balls, without a strike. O'Neill was at the point now where one good blow might make him fall apart at the seams.

When Stookey swung on the two-nothing pitch it looked for several long moments as though that blow had been delivered. It started on a low line, but built itself up and seemed to keep rising without sign of lessening its velocity. But a carrying wind from right field to left field suddenly took the big push out of it. It began to fade. Malison, in center field, was deep to his left now. He lunged and leaped at the same moment and, somehow, came down with the ball. Three runs, and maybe four, had just missed going into the Sox record book.

As the Sox bounded out of the dugout, Danny thought it would be some time before the team would put that many men on the bases, explode that much power, and fail to score even a single run. And, no question about it, you could charge it up to Fiske's badly timed delayed swing. Without that the Chiefs could well have been crushed completely in the first inning.

Somehow Danny didn't think he'd be sitting on that bench too much longer.

Chapter 11

IT HAPPENED SOONER THAN HE EXPECTED. THE MIST kept getting mistier and the slick outfield grass kept getting slicker. By the bottom of the sixth the umpires went into a huddle, holding palms toward the sky to gauge just how wet the world was. The crowd booed because the Chiefs were behind 5 to 4, and if the game was called they would be short-changed. And, what was just as important, so would the crowd—by three and one half innings of what they had paid good money to see.

The umpires decided the game would go on and a happy cheer went up. Phil Doyle was still in there for the Sox, though hanging off a cliff, and the same could be said for Bracken O'Neill. But outfield play had been affected by the weather; several hits might not have been hits on dry turf. Managers were consequently loath to flag the bull pen when you couldn't blame the troubles that arose entirely upon the man at the mound.

Lemmon, the left fielder, led off. He could hit a long ball. Doyle pitched him low, but too low. He went to three balls and one strike. Then he tempted Lemmon with a belt-high curve that broke sharply and Lemmon could not resist. But it was too much inside. Instead of pulling it toward the left-field seats, his obvious intention as he clobbered it, the ball veered far foul, distant and majestic and just plain strike two. On the mound Doyle looked slightly happy now after having looked badly frightened.

This time Doyle played it cozy with his prize pitch—a sinker. It was the pitch that had made him a good relief man before he had become a starter. It was a tough one to get in there on the three-and-two pitch, but Doyle made it. The trouble was, Lemmon made it too.

He slashed it, as was Doyle's intention, on the ground. But this ground ball dazzled Scalzi at third, as well it might. It almost knocked the third-base bag loose, squirted up into the air like a geyser. Scalzi caught it coming down as though it were a

pop fly, but of course it wasn't. It was a no-play infield hit.

Cutty Manganetti, the Chiefs' manager, came out
of the dugout as he called to Killiber, the next hitter.
Killiber walked back. He and Manganetti conferred, and the result of the conference immediately
became apparent upon Doyle's first pitch.

Killiber, the slugger, the home-run man, did not
try to pull the ball for the first time since Chief fans
could remember. He, like a hit-and-run artist of
long standing, delayed his swing and plugged the
ball on a soft line into right field. Because of Killiber's native power, his checked swing carried the
ball a greater distance than would have been the
case with a punch hitter. But it still looked good as
Fiske tore in after it. Meanwhile, Lemmon had
been off with the pitch.

The figure of Fiske became a blur in the mist. He
seemed to think he could reach it. He never stopped
running. He reached down to the shoetops, skidded,
and landed flat on his side. The ball shot by, roam-
ing toward the right-field corner with crazy twisting
action. Fiske was down and he couldn't seem to
get up.

It was a long run for Woodward from deep left

center, and by the time he caught up with the ball
and threw it in, even the slow-footed Killiber had
circled the bases. The Chiefs were in front, 6 to 5,
on the bloopiest home run any one had ever seen.
And Fiske was still on the ground.

Trainer and players rushed to him. Attendants
came out with a stretcher. Fiske waved the attendants away, and with one arm over Jake Brennan,
another over Eddie Lasky, he limped off the field
and into the tunnel.

Jug nodded at Danny. "You're in, Danny," he
said.

Danny went out and tossed a ball back and forth
with Woodward awhile, since Doyle was coming
out and Max Fitelson was coming in from the bull
pen. Doyle could hardly be blamed for the two runs,
but at the same time he'd been having an increasingly unsteady day.

Fitelson was a right-handed junk pitcher who
could deliver a very good job for an inning or two,
and sometimes even three. His earned-run average
had been right up at the top of the list for several
years—once as low as 1.78. He never looked like a
pitcher to be called on in the tight spot, but he got
the results. Now he scuffed the dirt, tugged at the

visor of his cap, wiped the back of his hand across his forehead. He always acted as nervous as a monkey on a stick and then proceeded to pitch as coolly as Warren Spahn facing the Married Men's team at a church picnic.

He coaxed Malison into a high, harmless sky-rocket shot to Jaffe in left. Banty, the catcher, drifted a foul fly behind the plate that Pete Gibbs swooped in, like a pickerel taking a minnow. Con-sala, the shortstop, hit to Fitelson and was out be-fore he was halfway to the bag.

But—the Sox had a deficit. One run.

Jaffe, Scalzi, and Stookey went down in order in the top of the seventh. So did the Chiefs in the bot-tom half. Pearson, Gibbs, and George Wettling—pinch-hitting for Fitelson—followed suit in the top of the eighth. Oklahoma Crane came in to pitch the bottom half of that inning.

Oklahoma, with his perennial control trouble, walked two Chiefs but he pulled out of the inning unscathed by a run. Now the Sox had their league-leading three-straight streak on the line, with the top of the batting order up.

Walker tried mightily with what was a long blast for him. It flew like a gull to deep left field, but he

wasn't Jaffe and the cross wind was still working.
Lemmon, back to the wall, pulled it in.

Danny set himself in the box for his first look at
Bracken O'Neill. O'Neill looked lazy out there, but
he had a sneaky fast pitch. And a nice change-up.
Danny disdained the first pitch, which was close.
The umpire called it a strike and he didn't argue.
He concentrated, as always, on the pitcher.

O'Neill broke one across his knees. He started
to go for it, then checked. A mistake. The ball hit
the outside corner for a clean strike and he knew it.
Now he was in the hole, in deep.

He knew it was usual for big-league pitchers to
think that rookies would be afraid to let a third
strike go by; that therefore they were suckers when
you got them in the hole. But he had the idea that
O'Neill was weary of throwing balls through the
damp mist and that this one would come in. He had
always been a hunch batter in the hole, because so
often his hunches had paid off.

And this one did. O'Neill came in with it. It was
on the outside edge of the plate—or would have
been. Danny stepped forward, into it, as he swung.
As usual, he went with the pitch and it sailed over
the first baseman's head, down the line. He made

his magically swift turn around the bag and went into second sliding, but really not needing to.

Now the free-swinging Woodward was up there. But O'Neill had a final burst of energy. He cut Woodward down with a slider that the big switcher popped high in the air over the mound. Killiber moved over and took it.

There was, finally, Jaffe left. Jaffe, with his hulking shoulders, refused to waste time. He took a ball and then he swung.

It was a shot through the box, streaking into center field. The trouble with Jaffe's singles was that they moved so fast they didn't leave a runner too much time to advance more than a base. But this was the tying run, the one they had to have, and Danny Redd's speed was known. Madigan, in the coaching box at third, was waving him on. He made the turn and kept on going.

Malison's throw was going to make it terribly close. He could tell that by the cry of the crowd and the look of the waiting Banty, blocking his path at the plate.

He had a choice. He could try to slide under Banty as he saw the catcher reach for the bounce of the throw; or he could crash him, full tilt, as he had a right to do, because Banty was in the base line, blocking the plate.

He went into the slide. He felt the tag. He heard the victorious roar of the crowd even before he saw the umpire's thumb jerked aloft. He jumped up, yelling at the umpire. Banty looked at him and laughed as he walked off. Danny saw the Sox trailing toward the tunnel. They saw no argument. He knew there was none.

It was clear that he'd made the wrong choice. The crash had been called for, not the slide. Banty had asked for it.

Chapter 12

DANNY TALKED THAT NIGHT, ALONE IN THE HOTEL room, with the only man on the team he trusted—Pete Gibbs. He talked about football, back in high school. He knew Pete had sort of steered him onto the subject, but he also knew that Pete never acted curious; rather, he showed a friendly interest; he gave the impression, always, that he wanted to help Danny.

"The football coach's name was Milt Skiff," he said. "He was all right except he was all football."

"I liked football in high school," Pete said. "I was an end. Second string, though."

"I didn't like it."

"How do you know if you never played it?"

"I knew I didn't like it just by watching it. Anyway, Milt Skiff heard about my speed. And my

brother Doug had played for Milt. Halfback. I saw
Doug carried off the field in two games. That was
enough for me."

"But Milt Skiff tried to get you out for the team?"

"He sure did. I used to play some touch football.
I liked that. I could pass good and run good. Milt
Skiff saw me one afternoon and he talked to me
about coming out for the team, the varsity no less."

"And you gave him a flat no."

"Pretty flat. I just told him I didn't go for that
blocking and tackling stuff. And I knew what my
brother was like after he got carried off the field
those two times."

"Your brother must be quite a guy."

"He's a PFC in the Army. And, last I knew, he
was a real drunk."

"He had tough breaks."

"Yeah. Something I don't want any part of. But
Milt Skiff, even though I said no, counted on me in
his plans for next fall. To be halfback, like Doug
had been."

"You didn't show on the field?"

Danny got out of the chair and went into the
bathroom for a drink of water. He wasn't used to

talking so much. He could only talk this way with
Pete Gibbs.

"I didn't even show at school," he said. "Not for
more than a week. About ten days, I think. I stayed
away that long just so I wouldn't have to go out for
football."

There was a silence, and then Pete said, "You're
a funny guy, Dan."

Nobody had ever called him Dan before. Just
Danny. He guessed because he'd been the younger
brother. Dan sounded more grown up, more like a
man than a boy.

"I guess so," he said. "But that's the way I am."

"You'll never be a big-leaguer playing ball that
way," Pete said.

"But I *am* a big-leaguer!"

"The season is four games old. There are a hundred and fifty more to go. If you're still around after
those are played then you can call yourself a big-
leaguer."

That ended the conversation and Danny was glad
of it. The morning paper convinced Danny further
that he was right, always had been, in his way of
playing ball. The special story about Chip Fiske

said that the veteran would be sidelined for the best part of a week because of a wrenched ankle.

"But I'll be back in that line-up, don't worry," Fiske was quoted as saying. "And when I get back in, I'll be back in to stay. I just don't see anybody around who can out hustle me for my job."

Spoken, Danny thought, like the typical never-say-die pro, who can't bear to admit that his time has come. He could see Fiske again, in his mind's eye, racing across the slippery turf and reaching down at full speed, skidding and crashing as the ball shot by. Under any circumstances, at Fiske's age, the ball should have been played for the legitimate single it had been; but on that mist-soaked turf trying for the shoestring had just been crazy heroics. Even the reporters hinted as much, though mildly, since everything they wrote about Fiske was tinged with respect and admiration for his scrappiness.

In the visiting team's dressing room Danny wasn't too surprised when Jug Slavin called him to the cubicle that passed as an office. He didn't seem to be in a very pleasant frame of mind as he spoke.

"The only reason I'm not fining you for letting

Banty block you off with the tying run and not doing anything about it is because that was the first time. Next time it will cost you a hundred."

"I thought I could make it by sliding past him."

Jug shook his head. "He had no business being in the base path. A catcher does that to you again, crash him. If you don't, then pretty soon every catcher in the league will do it, knowing you're a soft touch."

"I'll remember," Danny said.

"Fiske is out for a while so you're back in against any kind of pitching. That Fiske. . . ." Jug shook his head. "I don't say he did the smart thing on that shoetop miss on that wet turf, but I never criticize a player for too much hustle. Do you?"

"Of course not," Danny said. He didn't think Jug was really interested in his opinion on the matter; he thought Jug was just leading into something else he wanted to say.

"Because when one man on a team doesn't hustle enough, others have to hustle harder to make up for it. In a way, the man who dogs it endangers the others around him. They sometimes take risks they wouldn't, otherwise. Think about that, Redd."

Danny nodded, and Jug indicated that he'd said

everything that had been on his mind at the moment. It was with relief that Danny left him.

He became aware, as he changed from street clothes to uniform, that while a lot of conversation buzzed through the room none of it was directed his way. It made him realize that he was more of a loner than ever when Pete Gibbs wasn't around. But—that would change as he established himself, he felt sure.

Right then he was glad to be left alone with his thoughts. His conversations with Jug Slavin, he found, were becoming increasingly difficult for him. The trouble was that while he could listen to Jug, agree with him verbally, some part of his mind was always silently at work—and disagreeing.

He knew that he had talked freely with Pete Gibbs, more so than he ever had with anyone about things that went way back in his mind and memory. His brother being carried off the football field; his brother coming home from the bush leagues in defeat because of his injuries; his staying away from school so that he could avoid going out for the football team. But one thing he hadn't told Pete, so far, was that he had really tried to break out of this

strait jacket of fear many times in the minor leagues.
And failed.

There had been one night, back with the Colonials, when he could have saved a game with a catch
in the ninth at a time when enemy runners filled the
bases. He had seen, in his frantic pursuit of the
long drive, that he would have to risk crashing the
fence to get it. He'd made up his mind that he
would take that risk, get that ball, save that game
at any cost. But something had frozen in him as the
crucial moment came. He had not consciously quit
on the ball. But something, some protective instinct
that went deeper than his conscious thinking had
caused him to slow down just enough to avoid contact with the fence—and lose the ball and the ball
game for the Colonials.

That had happened so many times later on that
he came to realize he could not control himself in
those tight moments. And when he'd found he
couldn't seem to break the bonds that held him
back, he had turned on the whole idea and convinced himself that playing it safe was playing it
sensibly—that he believed in what he was doing.

Through the Sox farm system he had been able to
get away with these lapses of nerve. They had al-

ways been short on talent and, besides, the whole purpose of the farm system was to keep the talented prospects playing every day. But now, up here, he didn't think it would work out that way. So far Jug Slavin had not talked tough to him. But their relationship would keep getting more strained if he continued to give lip service to what Slavin said and did not follow it in action on the field. He wished he knew how to conquer the fear, or whatever it was, that blocked him in those crucial moments.

And yet, he could still tell himself with complete conviction that he was avoiding the mistakes that had wrecked his brother and Rip Radjecki and Pistol Pete Reiser and how many others? Sometimes he did not understand himself.

He was in uniform when Pete Gibbs finally arrived. Danny said, "What happened to you?"

"I stopped by the hospital."

"How was he?"

"Fine. Just mad at the doctor for making him stay there another day or two. If Chip had his way he'd be down here now. Probably volunteering to pitch batting practice."

Danny wanted to ask if Fiske had said anything about his failure to crash into Banty in the ninth.

But he held back. It would only look as though he were asking Pete to violate a confidence.

"Well," he said finally, "I'm glad to hear he's O.K. Jug told me I'm in there against any kind of pitching until he's back and ready."

Pete nodded. As he sat down and started to slip out of his slacks he gave Danny a sharp look, and said, "You'd better make hay, Dan. There's something about your style of play that seems to have made old Chip very confident he's going to get his job back. Full time, he thinks."

"We'll see," Danny said.

"That's what Fiske said," Pete told him.

Chapter 13

DANNY MADE HAY, TO USE PETE'S WORDS. HE MADE it fast and he made it big, to use his own words. And he just about wrapped up the right-field job, to use the sportswriters' words.

All this in a week. Against the Chiefs, in those last two games of the series, he went two for four and two for three and drew three bases on balls. He seemed to be on base every time a Chief pitcher turned around for a look. The hits included a double and a triple. He scored three runs and batted in three. He stole three bases. He nailed one runner at third on a long throw, another at the plate. He did not make an error. The need to crash a fence or a catcher never arose. The Sox took the series after losing that opener, and they moved on, a short hop, to the home park of the Robins.

The Robins were a new team in the league, replacing the old Grays. They were the second replacement in the league in the past two years. The first was out west, where the former, lowly Bears were now the Cougars and a team, according to forecast, to be reckoned with. Both teams had been made by franchise switching among cities. Danny decided that all the teams would look alike to him. He was feeling just right.

"Usually when a rookie catches on like this," one of the Blue Sox reporters wrote, "the old pros always say, 'Give him one turn around the circuit and the pitchers will begin to catch up with him.' Well, often that's true, but in this case we don't think so. They said that about Ted Williams and finally, after twenty or so years, the pitchers gave up the chase. In fact, everybody did except the opposition outfielders. Not that Danny Redd should properly be mentioned in the same breath with Williams, because he's not that type of ballplayer. He doesn't hit for distance too often but he *often* hits. If he doesn't hit he somehow wangles a walk. When he's on base, a pitcher gets fidgety, because you never know when Danny will take off. It does look, from

this corner—with the season only a week old—that
Danny Redd has it made."

Danny clipped that one out and kept it. All his
doubts and fears seemed to be getting resolved. He
went into the series with the Robins feeling sorry
for Chip Fiske, who took batting practice but did
not run much yet.

The Robins were a young team, almost all the way
down the line. Mostly farm-system products, not a
team built on trades and big-money buying. They
were expected to be tough this year, tough because
of good young pitching and a tight defense. They
were not a slugging band.

Oklahoma Crane pitched the opener for the Sox.
Jug Slavin was trying to build a Big Five instead of
a Big Four. If he found he could add Crane as a
starter, along with Lasky, Sloat, Rodriguez, and
Doyle it would mean that Lasky could get more
rest. At his age, thirty-nine, Lasky needed it. Crane
had everything that was required—fine speed, good
curve, nice change-up, even a slider. But consistent
control had so far eluded him.

Chico Astredos, a swarthy Latin member of the
Robins' young team, was their pitcher of the day.

Danny knew nothing about him, had never seen him before. Pete had said a lot of things about Astredos, but the one word that stuck in Danny's mind as he faced him, to open the game, was the word *crafty*.

Fortunately, Astredos couldn't seem to find the plate for three straight pitches. That was what Danny dearly loved—getting the pitcher so deep in the hole that the pressure was all a one-way proposition. Astredos threw a strike and Danny would have liked to come around on it. But a lead-off man simply didn't do that. Not with three and nothing.

He glanced down the line at Johnny Madigan. Madigan went through various traditional convolutions, but when Danny saw the left foot scuff dirt he knew he was free to swing away.

That fifth pitch came in across the letters, swift and straight, because Astredos needed the second strike and no doubt thought the speedy lead-off man would take it. But Danny didn't.

It was a "Redd Rider," as the reporters had started to call his line drives. It shot over third on a beeline to the base of the left-field foul pole. It stayed fair as it hit, then twisted deftly foul with Weedling, the Robins' left fielder, in discouraged pursuit.

Danny went into second standing up. There was no point in sliding, and reaching third base on a drive to left was out of the question. He called time and walked part of the way in to meet the visitors' bat boy and exchange the protective helmet for the regulation cap.

He could see he'd already built up a reputation among pitchers as a troublemaker on the bases. Astredos threw twice to Ransom, the rookie shortstop, who kept sneaking behind Danny as he took his full lead. Astredos shouted something in Spanish to which Ransom shouted "No dig!" and then called time to go over to the mound. Terandous, the big Greek catcher, went out to join them and the conference finally seemed to reach some sort of agreement.

Bud Walker was not going to bunt and the Robins knew it. They also knew that the scratchiest kind of an outfield single could very well bring Danny Redd home with a run. Astredos pitched Walker tight and he pitched him high, and found he was once more behind his hitter, two and nothing.

He came in with one on the outside corner and Walker went after it. But the ball did not go on a line. It flipped into the air, fairly high and fairly lazy and over the first baseman's head. Gentle, the Robins' first baseman, had a chance at it, though. He ran, back to the ball, taking a quick look over his shoulder. He almost reached the box-seat railing, pushed his bare hand out to hold himself away from it, and snared the ball in the webbing of his glove.

The roar of the crowd warned Danny. But it was too late. He had tagged up. He had taken off. Gentle had to release his bare hand from the railing, turn, get the ball out of his glove, then throw. By the time he threw Danny was one long jump from the third-base bag. But he knew he didn't have to jump. He just strolled in.

Madigan, in the coaching box, said, "Good jump on it, kid. Very fine indeed."

Roberson, the Robins' third baseman, said, mimicking Madigan, "Jump, indeed! He didn't need any jump. All he needed was a fast wheel chair."

"Don't come crying to us," Madigan told him.

Woodward slammed a long fly to dead center, and Danny trotted home. He had fixed the Sox up with a quick lead again. How many times in how many games? Fiske would have a cool summer waiting to get his job back again.

But that one run began to look sick in the last

half of the first inning. Oklahoma Crane could not find the plate. Not often enough, anyway. He walked the first two Robins, Brant and Weedling. Roberson bunted them to second and third. Gentle, on a three-and-nothing pitch, ripped a single to center and the Robins went ahead, 2 to 1.

But Crane settled down. So did Astredos. Each gave up a run in the fifth. The Sox got one in the sixth on a solo home run by Mike Jaffe. The Robins came back in the last of the seventh with back-to-back doubles by Terandous and Ransom.

Going into the top of the eighth, the Robins were leading, 4 to 3. Astredos still looked very much in charge. He sent Stretch Stookey, the first man up, down swinging. He muffled Andy Pearson with a deceptive change-up which Pearson popped sky high into the middle of the infield. Breening, the Robins' first-year kid on second base, took it with the suggestion of a yawn.

Now the Robins, sensing their man on the mound was getting stronger and therefore hoping for a quick slap down of the early-season Sox surge, talked it up like a bunch of blue jays in a worm farm.

Joe Rodriguez, from the Sox dugout, shouted something in Spanish, hands cupped, toward the mound. Whatever it was angered Astredos, and he pointed to the umpire behind the plate, then toward Rodriguez. The umpire had to shrug, because it was beyond his linguistic knowledge to know if Rodriguez had said anything wrong. This was a common problem with umpires, when Spanish-speaking ballplayers heckled each other. You could say that the Spanish-speaking ballplayer was almost safe from trouble that way.

Rodriguez' outburst seemed to have done the Sox no harm. Pete Gibbs promptly stung Astredos' first pitch into deep left center. It hit the wall, bounced around, and Pete went to second with a two-out double. The tying run.

Oklahoma Crane, who had pitched a game good enough to win most of the time, had to come out. In his place Jug sent up Frank Palaski, a rookie catcher, second only to Gibbs. Palaski batted left-handed and had power.

Palaski didn't look graceful. He batted from a crouch, and always looked as though he would up-percut the ball. The crouch made him difficult to pitch to, because he was short and stocky, like Berry of the Clippers. Astredos, who had never seen him before, could not get the ball into the tight little groove which Palaski seemed to leave for a strike zone. He walked on four pitches. Danny moved in.

His first-inning double had been his only hit off Astredos, but he had hit two other solid balls, though straight at fielders. And he had walked once. Now Astredos, looking suddenly harried, missed the first pitch. He caught a low outside corner on the second one. Count all even. He threw high on the third one. Danny swung at the next.

He knew it was sweet when it left the bat. He had gone with the pitch as usual, and now it found its way between right and center. He never lessened speed around second as he saw Madigan pulling him on with his arms, saw Gibbs crossing the plate, Palaski close behind. He slid into third with no trouble, and the Sox were in front, 5 to 4.

That was all for Astredos. Boyd Wolheim, a master of the butterfly ball, came in from the bull pen. He retired Walker on a ground ball to Roberson.

Now, Danny thought, as he went out to position, "I've *really* got it made. This nails it down."

It seemed to. Brant struck out. Weedling singled to center. Roberson grounded to Stookey, Weedling taking second. Then Gentle came up, the big third out. Gentle hit left-handed and he hit a long ball

sometimes. Danny played him to pull; so did Woodward. Jaffe played left as though for a straightaway
hitter. If Gentle took a late swing, a left fielder had
a lot of ground to cover.

Gentle took two balls, then a strike. After that
he made his move. Max Fitelson, who had replaced
Oklahoma Crane, made one a little too good. Gentle
laced it.

The ball was headed on a rising line to that
dreaded pocket between right and center. This time,
Danny thought, I won't slow down. I won't. I will
get this ball.

It was surely his. Woodward stood a ghost of a
chance, but only that. It was in Danny's territory.
He kept going, seeing the ball losing height, coming
down. He hadn't lessened speed when he heard
Woodward yell, "Me! *Me!*"

Woodward was crazy. Or else Woodward
thought that he, Danny Redd, would quit on it
again. He would have to show Woodward this time.
Show them all.

"I've got it!" he screamed. *"Got it!"* And this
time he did not slow down. This time his eye never
left the ball, never searched for the wall. Or for
Woodward.

He felt the ball hit his glove the moment he felt the crash. He didn't know if it was the wall or Woodward. It happened too fast. Rockets went off before his eyes and a roaring in his ears turned into cathedral silence. He did not know, as he ceased hearing and ceased seeing, whether he held the ball or not.

Chapter 14

WHEN HE WOKE UP, HE KNEW HE WAS IN A HOSPITAL by the blurred white look all around him. And through the blur he saw faces, dimly. When they began to look clear to him, he recognized Pete Gibbs, Russ Woodward, Jug Slavin. Behind them he recognized Rip Radjecki talking to Doc Dougherty.

Pete Gibbs first saw that his eyes were open. Pete said, "You awake now, Dan?"

Danny started to nod, but that hurt his head. "What did I hit—the wall or Woodward?" he asked.

"Woodward," said Woodward.

"Did I hold the ball?"

Jug Slavin shook his head. "Who could?"

"Then the run came in," Danny said. "It tied up the game."

"We won in the twelfth," Slavin said.

Danny shut his eyes again. He was glad to hear that. He would hate to think he had gone through all this for a lost ball game. After a few moments he realized that Woodward didn't seem to be hurt at all. He opened his eyes again and looked at Woodward.

"How did you make out?" he asked.

"I was lucky," Woodward said. "And, of course, I've got quite a few pounds on you. My shoulder's sore. That's about all."

Danny next glanced at Doc Dougherty. "How long have I been out?"

John Dougherty, who always said his one claim to fame was that he had been All-Star first baseman in the Medical School softball league, came over by the bed.

"Not long," he said. "But then, you had sedatives. That was early last evening. You see, Danny, you suffered a slight concussion."

"That's all?"

"No. A collarbone complication. Not broken. But it needs some mending."

All this sounded bad to Danny. He could have been another case like his brother or Radjecki. Just on one move, one slight slip from his usual way of playing ball. Of course, it had been Woodward's fault. The ball had not been in Woodward's territory in the first place. And as soon as he thought that, he realized why Woodward had kept coming: Woodward had thought he would play it safe the way he had played Skanran's home-run out in that first game at the Stadium. That time Woodward had left it to him; this time Woodward had been afraid to. He saw that it had been his own pattern of play that had put him here on a hospital bed.

Radjecki came over then and his face, for the first time, looked really friendly. "I know it's tough and I know you're hurting," he said. "But, Danny, you surely did look like a real big-league outfielder."

Danny turned his head away, afraid he might reply to the friendly look with a black scowl. It dawned on him as Radjecki finished speaking that they all thought he had become some kind of a brand new ballplayer in that instant of collision and blackout. They all thought he would now turn into Rip Radjecki, Pistol Pete Reiser, and Country Slaughter, rolled into one.

Boy, were they wrong! That instant had been the

first time he had ever conquered the fear that had held him back. And now, coming out of it, he knew the fear was worse than it had ever been; he knew that if it took that kind of football heroics to impress them, he just had no desire to impress them.

The next time, Woodward could get the ball—if it came to such a decision. And just to prove he was right he looked at Doc Dougherty and asked, "How long before I climb back into the uniform?"

"It all depends, Danny," Dougherty said. "Certainly not for a couple, maybe three, weeks."

"Three weeks!" he said. Why, in three weeks Fiske could have the job all sewed up. Or some rookie punk from the farm system could be called up and *he* could have it sewed up.

"That's why," Jug Slavin said, "after getting Doc Dougherty's opinion in the matter, we've put you on the temporarily disabled list. But the season's young, son."

For a moment he couldn't reply. His tongue stuck to the roof of his mouth. When you were put on the temporarily disabled list, it meant you were not eligible to play again for thirty days.

He looked around at these people who were here

to pay some sort of homage, show him some deep respect. For what? Angrily he thought, for being a boob. For momentarily rejecting the code of safety that had brought him up, unharmed, to the big leagues. In one quick fraction of a second he had destroyed all his carefully laid plans; in that instant he had gambled away the future—the fame and the money—that he knew his talent could bring him.

He didn't feel like a hero at all. He felt like a guy who ought to have his head examined—what there might be left of it. In thirty days, if the Sox were moving smoothly, he could find himself back in Rapid City. "On twenty-four-hour option, of course," the front office would say. "We think you just need to get your eye back, your timing back."

Often, too often, that was the last the big leagues ever heard of a rookie who made a quick splash in April. He had been a fool, but if he ever pulled out of this mess he had let himself in for he would never be that kind of fool again.

"What do I do meanwhile?" he asked. "Watch television?"

"For the present," Doc Dougherty said, "just stay as sweet as you are."

Dougherty grinned and Danny had to grin back. After all, he wasn't sore at the doc. He wasn't sore, even, at Woodward. His target was himself.

He looked at Jug Slavin. "I guess somebody takes my place for thirty days, Mr. Slavin?"

"Make it Jug, Danny," Slavin said. "Yes. Naturally. There's got to be somebody to go along with Fiske. At his age you never know. We're bringing up a boy from Rapid City. You saw him in spring training. Duke Page."

"I remember him," Danny said thoughtfully. "He used to play in left field."

Jug nodded. "He's been playing right field at Rapid City."

Well, Danny thought, Duke Page is a big, strong, eager boy. He can muscle a ball. But he's not too fast, his arm is just so so, and he isn't really ready yet.

"I think," Doc Dougherty said, "the warrior should get some more sleep."

As Dougherty handed him a glass of water and a pill, Danny waved at his visitors. "Thanks for the burial," he said.

"What in the world do you mean by that?" Pete Gibbs asked.

"Slip of the tongue," Danny said. "I meant, thanks for coming up. Thanks for everything. Thanks a lot."

But no thanks, he thought, to himself.

Chapter 15

THIRTY DAYS IS AS LONG A STRETCH OF TIME AS YOU want to make it. Danny somehow managed to make it the longest.

He spent a week in the hospital. By that time the eastern clubs had finished their games in the east and had headed west. He lived at the hotel, but went every second day to see Doc Dougherty for treatment of the collarbone. With a TV set in the hotel room he could watch some of the games that were sent back; he listened to the radio broadcasts of the ones that were not. Gradually his bitterness subsided, because what was happening to the Blue Sox was heartening to Danny Redd.

Not that Danny rooted against Fiske and Duke Page, who were alternating in right field. But he could not honestly feel any sorrow when they did

[125]

something in the field or at the plate which failed
to help the Blue Sox pennant cause. These things
happened with some frequency.

When Page played, he batted seventh behind
Pete Gibbs, who had been shoved up from eighth
to sixth, while Stookey had been switched from
sixth to second, behind Walker, who now led off. In
the games when Fiske played right field, the whole
order underwent a shake-up, since Fiske hit second
and Stookey dropped back to sixth. It became a
jumble from day to day, that Sox batting order, and
this was something that Jug Slavin had always tried
to avoid.

The Sox were not doing extra well after that fast
start. They lost the first western series to the Panthers, two out of three. They broke even, one and
one, with the Redskins after a rained-out first game.
They were grand-slammed by the revived Cougars,
and that was when the Robins slipped past them
into first place, while the Clippers moved up even.

By the time they came back home no team in the
league looked too bad, but no team acted as though
it "was the team to beat," as the reporters liked to
put it. The Robins were still clinging to first place,
by a game. The Clippers were second. The Sox

were two behind the Clippers, and both the Redskins and Cougars were breathing on their necks.

Fiske, Danny noted in the Sunday paper's full
league batting averages, was hitting .256. Duke
Page was hitting .271. Neither had distinguished
himself in the field, any more than at bat. Both, according to the broadcasters Danny listened to and
the reporters he read, were giving it the full battle
for the job. But Duke Page, he knew, was a left
fielder and not a right fielder. When he was in there,
runners on first took liberties on a single to right
field and usually wound up on third base. When
that happened too often a manager was always
worried.

In addition, Danny knew that when he was in
there, an authentic lead-off man, Jug Slavin had a
balanced batting order, one he could stick to. And
that was something Jug had always liked.

Danny had read how Jug had stayed with his line-
up more than most managers. They called him the
Patient Man and said that once he had made a final
decision he stayed with it, because he had so much
self-confidence in his decisions. The reporters said
it took self-confidence to be a patient man, and that
sounded to Danny like the straight scoop.

This, he considered, the biggest single factor in his favor with Jug. Jug liked a balanced line-up and he couldn't have one this year without Danny Redd playing right field and leading off for the Sox.

Then the team came home, flying in Sunday night, and Doc Dougherty gave Danny the word he could work out every day. But lightly at first. He had another week to go before the thirty days were up.

So long Duke Page, Danny thought.

There was a wonderful feeling about being back in the Stadium, stomping the turf again, even though he knew he could not get back into the line-up for seven more days. After early salutations from a bunch around the Coke cooler in the dressing room, Danny hurried into uniform and went onto the field early, along with the utility players.

After mild participation in a pepper game, he started throwing back and forth with Willie the Lion. The Lion, who spent his whole baseball life in the bull pen, was always looking for exercise. "Man," he said to Danny, holding his overpadded mitt for the throw, "we sure missed you on that trip. Don't like that west, anyway. Never did like the west. Vibrations all wrong out there."

"Guess you'd never make a cowboy," Danny said, grinning at the Lion's highly expanded waistline.

"If I got on a horse I'd flatten him down," the Lion said. "I wouldn't do it to a horse. But we missed our speedy boy. Know what I told a reporter out there in that west?"

"What?"

"I said you were the fastest man in the league. I said that if I raced you to first base and you ran backwards you would beat me by five steps."

"Want to try?" Danny asked.

"Confidentially, but don't tell Mr. Slavin, I can't run that far."

When batting practice started, Danny took his cuts and took them in his accustomed place—first. He watched Duke Page swing and saw that Page could belt them. But he wasn't worried about Page right now. For seven days he didn't have anything to worry about except getting loose and limber.

He shagged balls during batting practice for a while. But he didn't chase them. The ones he could reach by moving at a slow pace he caught. The others he let roll.

He watched infield practice and felt a thrill that he was on such a team. The precision, the authority, the happy certainty of every move was a picture. Madigan had the bat and Gibbs stood by his side with the mitt. Madigan slapped one down the line to Scalzi. Scalzi stabbed as it took the crucial bounce, plucked it out of the pocket as he turned toward first, then fired it to Stookey. Stookey's glove swallowed it as he touched toe to bag and then he rammed it down to Gibbs, who rammed it back to Scalzi at third. Scalzi shot it back across to Stookey and then it zoomed into Gibbs' mitt. He flopped it, without even looking into Madigan's waiting and open palm.

The dizzy progress of the ball continued endlessly, with never a flicker of a fumble. Meanwhile balls were flying back and forth over the infielders' heads, to and from the outfield as Radjecki and the Lion belted flies with fungo bats. There was as much going on as took place in a three-ring circus, yet everything was orderly and exact. The word for it was—pro.

Finally the umpires arrived and the infield was swept. Jug Slavin emerged from the dugout and was met at home plate by Jocko Dikes, manager of the Panthers. They went through the familiar but necessary routine of ground rules they all had known for many years. Then the Sox sprang out of the dugout and charged to positions. Lury, a right-hander, was pitching for the Panthers today. So Fiske was in right field. Danny picked his towel from the hook behind him in the dugout and wiped the perspiration. Then he leaned back against the dugout wall. He had seven games to watch the other people do it. After that he'd pick up where he had left off.

Never, never again would he play Radjecki's game. From here on in he would play Danny Redd's game. The hospital and then the bench—it was not his idea of a big deal. Let the heroes have it.

Chapter 16

THE DAY DANNY CAME OFF THE DISABLED LIST HE
learned that right field was a three-man fight. It had
been natural to expect that Duke Page would be
shipped back to Rapid City now that the need for
him was over. That didn't happen.

Instead, the Sox asked waivers on the veteran
Buck Riordan, an outfielder whose only use had become that of a pinch hitter. The Cougars promptly
claimed Riordan for the waiver price and that left
the Sox with three right-field specialists: Redd,
Fiske, and Page. It was what the reporters called a
dogfight, Danny thought. Except that he, Danny
Redd, had the special talent the Sox needed. Fiske
had had it once, but no more. Page didn't have it
and never would. Page was a hustler, but he didn't

have speed and he never would hit for percentage—
not in a class with Danny Redd, anyway.

Danny made his comeback in style, he thought.
The Cougars were closing out their three-day visit
and this was the rubber game of the series. The
weekday crowd wasn't large, but the fans gave
Danny a tremendous hand when he trotted out to
right field. And he gave them a quick tip of his cap.

He showed them what they had been missing in
that first inning of his return. There was one out,
Cougars on first and third. The hitter, left-handed,
pulled one down the right-field foul line. It was
fairly deep—deep enough for the runner on third to
tag up.

Danny held back just enough as he came in on the
ball to meet it at the height of his onrush, in a direct
line with the plate. The impetus of his rush was in
the flight of the ball as it left his hand. It hit the
infield skin a few yards in front of Pete Gibbs,
planted at the plate, then skimmed into his big mitt.
He had the runner, sliding, with seconds to spare.

The ovation for Danny when he trotted in to the
dugout was the sweet sound of old times. As he went
to the bat rack he passed Gibbs, taking off the
clumsy tools of his trade. "After that strike," Pete

said, "I wouldn't be surprised if the Skipper called you in to relieve, should Sloat get himself in a jam."

"They used to do that to me on the sand lots," Danny said.

"With an arm like that maybe it's too bad it turned out you could hit."

"Someday I'll show you my fuzz ball," Danny told him.

"Why do you call it that?"

"Because it's peachy," Danny said, and jumped out of the way as Gibbs threw his mitt at him.

It was a good feeling to have Gibbs heave the mitt at him over his bad joke. In a funny way it made him feel Gibbs' equal, as a regular. Regulars didn't indulge in horseplay with any teammates except those they considered their equals. Danny had noticed that fact in spring training.

The Cougars' pitcher was Johnny Kecks, who was a product of the Clipper farm system. The Clippers and the Cougars had made so many deals since the shift of the Bear franchise that the wags sometimes referred to this new team as a Clipper farm club. Nevertheless, they had picked up a lot of good young ballplayers in return for a few established veterans in the past couple of years.

Kecks missed on a fast ball, then caught a corner with a slow curve. He missed again on the fast ball. Danny was in no rush to swing. He took a change-up for a second strike. Once more Kecks tried to calibrate his fast ball. This time he succeeded—and Danny blessed him.

The ball left his bat with the true sound of a line drive going somewhere definite. This one went down the left-field line with such rapidity that Seeburn, covering that section for the Cougars, hardly seemed to see it until it tore the turf. Danny went into second base with no contest.

The Redd ovations grew louder. Lampe, the Cougar second baseman, said, "I hear you got a new collarbone. Plastic?"

"Yeah," Danny said. "I got it free, just by sending a bunch of box tops."

"Good deal," Lampe said, and returned to position.

Danny liked that talk, too. It meant he had been discussed. If you were discussed by other teams, that meant they figured you would be around awhile.

Walker grounded to second and Danny went to third with no fuss about it. Woodward slashed a sizzling ground ball that completely tied Thornboro, the Cougar first baseman, into knots. When he managed to untangle himself and throw to Kecks, covering the bag, Woodward was so long past it that he could have had time to autograph a score card in the first-base box seats had he so chosen. The official scorer had to call it a hit. When a ground ball moved with that velocity, a first baseman was lucky to remain physically undamaged.

Danny was thinking, as he dropped into the dugout, that Woodward ought to love him; over a full season he would be on base so many times when Woodward came up that the big center fielder should be a shoo-in for the RBI title.

Jaffe singled to left, Scalzi belted a triple off the left-center wall, and Stookey walked. That was the end of Kecks for the day. Ned Graver, who followed Kecks, managed to throw a zip-zip-zip double-play ball to Andy Pearson, so the Sox had to settle for three runs.

It was all they needed, as matters turned out. The final score was 7 to 1, and the Cougars left town with their dreams of a first-division finish considerably tarnished.

After Danny rode back to the hotel with Pete

Gibbs, he was alone in the lobby when Charlie Kendall, a reporter he knew, dropped down in the
leather chair next to his. "A good game, Danny,"
he said.

"Thanks." It had been, all in all. Double, infield single, walk. Five put-outs. One assist. You
couldn't possibly knock it. He had to agree with
Kendall.

"The idea is prevalent," Kendall said, "that you
are a changed man."

Danny looked at him. He liked the idea of being
called a man instead of a boy or a lad or one of those
words that always sounded so superior. But the
question sounded loaded; he had talked to enough
sportswriters to know by now that in the hope of
creating a story they would ask questions which
managers always called "loaded." He felt wary and
thought about this one. "How do you mean—
changed?" he asked finally.

Kendall, whom Danny remembered as the only
reporter he knew who didn't smoke, brought out a
package of gum and offered a stick. Danny shook his
head, after a look; he was fussy about flavors.

"I mean," Kendall said, "you have the reputation

of a player who . . . well . . . takes care of himself. On the field and off."

"I learned that at the Y.M.C.A.," Danny informed him.

"What I mean is," Kendall said, pausing to tuck the stick of gum in his mouth, "you never did anything to get yourself hurt until that collarbone accident. Running into Woodward."

"That won't happen again," Danny said.

"Why not?"

"Because I won't let it," Danny said. He looked up and saw Pete Gibbs walking over. He was glad. It was time to eat and he didn't want to answer any more questions. You could make a big mistake if you talked too freely to the sportswriters sometimes. He knew. He'd made a number of such mistakes in the past.

He arose. "Here's my roomie," he said to Kendall. "Time to put on the feedbag. See you."

Kendall arose and nodded. "I just want to be sure of one thing, Danny. Have I got it right? Did you say, quote, *that won't happen again,* unquote?"

"Yes. Sure. Why?"

"Because I like to be exact when I quote," Kendall said, and he wandered off.

Pete Gibbs had arrived and he looked after Kendall. "What was his angle this time?" he asked.

"There wasn't any angle," Danny said. "He just sort of complimented me on my game today."

"Well, good for Kendall," Gibbs said. He kept staring after the reporter. "He must have turned over a new leaf."

"He didn't bother me at all," Danny told him.

Chapter 17

IT WAS THE LAST OF THE EIGHTH INNING. THE RED-
skins were holding tenaciously to a 3 to 2 lead. They
had held that lead since the first inning in which
they had scored their three runs and the Sox had
scored their two. New pitchers came in during that
first inning. The relievers had been good. They had
been Steegman, a left-hander, for the Redskins; Oklahoma Crane for the Sox.

After seven and a half innings of almost no move-
ment on the base paths, the Sox seemed suddenly
to explode in their next-to-last chance to pull this
one out of the fire.

Gibbs opened the bottom of the eighth with a
Texas league single to center. That brought up Chip
Fiske to pinch-hit for Oklahoma Crane. Fiske tried
to bunt Gibbs to second, but he only succeeded in

forcing Gibbs at that bag. Immediately the youthful, springy Duke Page was sent in to run for the elderly Fiske.

Page danced off first and on the third pitch to Danny Redd he lit out. Because Redd had sliced an outside pitch to right field, Page had no trouble going into third base as there was no throw. Redd remained on first.

The crowd, sensing a lost cause turned into victory, stood up as it yelled. Joe Gardnan, the Redskin manager, strolled out of the dugout. His stroll indicated he was not yanking Steegman, but just wanted to settle him down with some careful words. Even so, the broadcasters in the booths reported solemnly—as though coining a gem of a phrase— that there was activity in the Redskins' bull pen.

Gardnan went back to the dugout and Steegman was once more left to his own resources. He got one strike on Walker and then missed the zone in four subsequent endeavors. Walker trotted cheerfully down to first, the bases were loaded, one out. Gardnan put his trust in Steegman all the way, not making a move from the dugout shade.

Steegman tried. He did not rattle. He ran the switch-hitting Woodward (now batting right-handed) to the full count. And then he threw the ball that separated the men from the boys.

He discovered what he had previously suspected —Woodward was no boy. Woodward's line drive to the left-field wall was so vicious, so hard, that Danny Redd on second base turned, startled. It had been hit so low there seemed a good chance it would be caught. He hesitated between second and third.

The drive rammed the wall and ricocheted with such force that Purcell, the Redskins' fine center fielder caught it on the fly—off the fence.

What happened after that became garbled in the morning papers. The consensus, after many interviews with the players concerned, was this:

Duke Page, running for Chip Fiske, came in easily to score the tying run. Danny Redd, transfixed between second and third like a politician waiting for the results from the outlying precincts in an election, finally saw the ball had not been caught. He ran into third, was waved on by Madigan, and then saw that his delay had trapped him.

Perhaps not. But perhaps so. At any rate, the Redskins' catcher, Ramono, was blocking the path. Ramono was blocking it just as unfairly as Banty had blocked it on Danny Redd in the series with the

Chiefs. Danny realized the word had got around to the catchers in the league. He further realized that he had two quick courses of action. He could crash into Ramono or he could hastily retreat to third base and wait there for a less strenuous way to get the winning run in. He chose to turn and shoot back to third base.

But Walker had not hesitated on his start from first base when Woodward had clobbered the ball. Seeing Danny Redd trapped between third and the plate, thanks to Purcell's deadly accurate throw, he plunged on to the bag.

Complications piled upon complications. Woodward, running like the human deer that he was, vaguely saw someone trapped between third and the plate. But he thought it was Walker, assuming that the speedster, Danny Redd, had long since scored. It was inconceivable to him that Redd had not scored on such a mighty blow.

As a result, Woodward piled into third base. And so there were three Blue Soxers at the same base: Redd, Walker, and the falsely confident Woodward.

Traffic conditions were terrible, but were easily straightened out. Walker, seeing that Redd had a chance to make it back to the bag, and realizing he now had no future as a base runner in this inning, politely stepped aside to give the faster man the chance to stay alive.

As he did this, Woodward, who knew nothing except that he had hit an authentic triple, passed Walker, officially, on the base paths. Having passed Walker, he was immediately out for long-honored technical reasons. Walker, startled beyond reason at what had transpired, was quickly tagged.

Thus the net result of Woodward's bases-loaded triple was one run, an official two-base hit, and a double play at third base. Years later when fans who saw it were not believed by listeners, they could only fall back on the old defense: you could look it up.

Danny got his glove without looking at anybody and went out to right field. He heard unfriendly sounds behind him. He heard definite words after that.

"The gutless wonder!"

"Never hurt the catcher, old buddy!"

"Take good care of yourself, sonny boy!"

It wasn't nice to hear. What made it worse was that the Redskins squeezed a run across in the top of the ninth and that was the ball game.

In the dressing room later no one was talking to him. Not even Pete Gibbs. Pete had somehow made himself scarce. And when Jug finally called him to his office, he wasn't surprised. He was relieved—to get it over with.

Radjecki was there, too. Jug said, "A couple of things to talk over, Danny. Not the ball game first. *This* first."

He thrust the sports page of an afternoon newspaper at Danny. He looked. The heading of the Charlie Kendall story said: *It Won't Happen Again —Danny Redd*. A quick glance at the opening showed him that Kendall had built quite a story out of their conversation. The point of it seemed to be that Danny Redd had meant he would never take a risk again, no matter what the situation of the game might be. He looked up.

"Well?" Jug asked. And Radjecki, silent, was asking the same question with his eyes.

Chapter 18

DANNY DIDN'T KNOW WHAT TO SAY. HE HAD READ enough of the Kendall story to see that it was one of those cases where a reporter had blown a story up out of all proportion. But at the same time Kendall had not misquoted him. Kendall had sensed the truth of his attitude. He glanced back at the paper again and his words came back to haunt him.

"You never did anything to get yourself hurt until that collarbone accident—running into Woodward," I said to Danny Redd.
Redd replied, "That won't happen again."
I asked, "Why not?"
"Because I won't let it," Redd told me.

"Sometimes," he heard Jug saying, "these reporters do misquote. They've misquoted me often. I can understand how that happens especially with a rookie who hasn't learned the art of dodging those loaded questions. Did Kendall misquote you, Danny?"

"No, he didn't," Danny answered.

Jug banged the open palm of his hand down on top of his head. "And just to make Kendall's story the scoop of the season you had to throw away a ball game Woodward won for us out there this afternoon—to prove that the quotes were right."

Danny knew that something inside him was close to boiling over. He said angrily, "Ramono had me trapped. . . ."

"He was in the base path, just as Banty was that time. You had every right to bowl the guy over like a tenpin. Knowing that two men were flying around the bases behind you, there was positively no excuse for you to quit cold and beat that retreat to third base."

"I didn't think of all that at the time."

"You thought about yourself," Jug said. "About protecting yourself at the expense of the team. Never, *never* in my life has a team of mine been turned into a national joke. And if you don't think the Blue Sox are a national joke after that caper, read the papers tomorrow. Three men on third! A double play on a bases-loaded triple! They don't play baseball *that* bad on the sand lots!"

He arose and walked to the window. He seemed unable to contain himself for the moment. Danny looked forlornly at Rip Radjecki. He'd had no idea of the size of the catastrophe he seemed to have created.

Radjecki finally spoke. "Danny," he said, "I told you a hundred years ago that you can't be a big-leaguer with a touch-football player's attitude. *When* are you going to find out?"

Then there was silence—heavy and prolonged. Jug turned back to the desk. He looked as puzzled and unhappy as a hound dog suddenly locked alone inside a car. "I told you when you let Banty block you that way it would cost you a hundred the next time. Well—it's costing you a hundred this time."

Danny nodded.

Jug went on. "There's dissension on this team now. I can smell it from here to the shower stalls. The others have resented it, each time you didn't go all out—meaning, you let them down. But now. . . ." He shook his head.

Danny went to the door, paused, and turned

around. "Just one thing I want to say, I've helped win more ball games than I've helped lose in the little time I've played."

"That's not the point!" Jug said sharply. "The point is you only help win them when it doesn't cost you anything. And sometimes it's got to cost to win in baseball like in just about everything else."

He turned his back and Danny moved fast. No word was spoken to him by anyone as he finished dressing for the street. There was still no sign of Pete Gibbs. He walked out alone and decided to splurge on a taxi, all by himself. Unless you chipped in with three or four other players it was an expensive ride from the Stadium to the hotel. But in his mood he didn't want to tangle with the subway crowd and he didn't want to talk with anybody on the team.

As he waited at the curb to flag a cab two small boys wandered past and stared in sudden recognition. One pointed his finger at Danny and said to the other, "It's Danny Redd! It's the guy who was afraid to go home!"

"You sure loused *that* game up!" the second one jeered.

Just then a cab stopped and Danny was grateful

to jump inside. Fortunately, the driver did not seem
to recognize his face. But he had the radio turned
on, listening to a postgame sports report. The voice
of the broadcaster struck Danny's ears with the
sound of gravel rolling down a chute.

And while the Blue Sox achieved fame of a certain
sort this afternoon, it's not the kind of fame they're
used to—or that will ever get anybody concerned into
the Hall of Fame. Reliable sources have informed
this sportscaster that two conferences are about to
be held within the Blue Sox ranks and both of them
concern the future of their brightest rookie in years—
Danny Redd. Conference Number One will be between Manager Jug Slavin and General Manager
Stan Davis. Conference Number Two will be held
between the Blue Sox player-representative of the
pension fund, Pete Gibbs, and the rest of the Sox
personnel. There is no question that Redd has become more than a mere rookie problem to the Sox;
he has become a serious issue in terms of team har-
mony. Gibbs is in the unfortunate position of being
both the duly elected spokesman for the players in
all matters to which they are entitled to a voice, and
also the roommate and closest friend of the top man
on the seesaw. Just how this Danny Redd problem
will be figured out is difficult to guess and I won't.

The fact remains that Redd is loaded with all-around baseball talent, he's the answer to the crying need the Sox have had for a lead-off man, and the scouts have all said he can't miss being a sure .300 hitter. But how much does all that mean when you have a team and a following of fans up in the air with resentment over his lack of hustle—a lack brought out so dramatically this afternoon that. . . .

"Will you turn that thing off?" Danny asked the driver.

"Sure," he said, and did. "I never see a ball game in four, five years now. But drivin' this hack around all day I tune in on the games, just for company. You see the game today?"

"Yes," Danny said.

"This kid, Danny Redd," the driver said, "must have a shingle loose somewhere."

Danny didn't reply.

Chapter 19

Danny ate early and alone. Then he went right up to the room after buying a paperback mystery. He wanted to read so that he wouldn't think, and he knew that if he read the papers he would read about himself. Three times, while he was still on the first chapter of the mystery, the phone rang. Each time it was a reporter who wanted to come up and talk to him; each time Danny said no, positively no. He doubted that he would ever talk to a reporter again.

He was on the third chapter when Pete Gibbs walked in. He took a quick, anxious look at Pete's face and he didn't like what he saw. There weren't many people he had known well who were as amiable and friendly as Pete had been. Now Pete looked stern, stern as a schoolteacher who has caught somebody cribbing on an exam. It came to him, suddenly, how much Pete's friendship meant to him and how freely it had been given. But at this moment Pete did not look like a friend.

"I've got to tell you something," Pete said, "not as a roommate, friend, or adviser, but as the players' representative who has to say something that is official."

"I heard on the radio that there was a meeting," Danny said. He looked away from Pete after he spoke.

"There was a meeting, yes," Pete said. "I called it."

"*You* called it? Why *you?*"

"Because there's a nice little package of gold at the end of the pennant chase, and the whole team just could share in it. But we need to like each other or we'll never make it. And I know how much resentment there is over you. I don't need to tell you why that resentment exists."

"I wish you'd cut this short," Danny said. "I've been listening to nothing but this stuff for the last couple of hours."

"All right, short it is. We took a vote on whether we wanted to gamble our very possible world series money on you or on Fiske and Page. The vote went against you."

Danny knew that if he made any reply his voice would crack on him. He remained silent.

"All the vote means," Pete said, "is that it will be reported to Jug and to the front office. It proves nothing beyond expressing the players' sentiments to the people higher up, who have the final decision in these things."

Danny knew he couldn't stay in this room much longer. He stood up. "Only one question, Pete— how did *you* vote?"

"I voted for you, Danny," he said. "But you might as well know—I was the only one who did."

"Well, if you're the head man, I mean the player-representative is the head man. . . ."

"I'm not the player-representative any more," Pete said. "Eddie Lasky is. Since I was the only one who backed you up I figured I wasn't very representative of the club's feelings."

"You—you resigned over *me?*" Danny said.

"They were all pretty mad at me for voting against their solid sentiments. I could understand it."

Danny had never felt quite so overwhelmed by

a friendship. He had never had a friend who had gone so far out on a limb for him. He didn't know what to say and the silence grew awkward. "Pete. . . ." He tried to grope for words but it was no use.

"It's not easy to say this to you, Danny," Pete cut in, seeing his embarrassment. "But the team resents you now. In lots of ways you and I can't blame them. When a ballplayer plays for money, big money that involves more than twenty others and their families too, well, he's cheating unless he gives anything less than his best."

Danny saw Pete's face in a sort of blur, as though there was a fog in the room. Then Pete went over to the door and opened it. He said, over his shoulder, "See you tomorrow. I've been invited to stay with friends, across town. There's an old pal I haven't seen in a long time. . . ."

He shut the door. Danny stood there looking at it. He didn't believe Pete's story about the old pal and the invitation across town. He just knew Pete thought it was better that they didn't talk about it any more tonight.

Danny didn't sleep much that night, and when he went to the Stadium late the next morning he took his suitcase with him. He had an idea he would be cleaning out his locker before the end of the afternoon. Once Jug Slavin and the general manager heard about that player vote—well, it was bound to show them that having Danny Redd around was the same as having trouble around.

Chapter 20

THE FIRST THING HE DID WHEN HE REACHED THE dressing room was to stuff the suitcase, end up so that it fitted, into the locker. No one had seen him with the suitcase except Pickles, the clubhouse man. No one else had arrived yet except Pickles, and Danny had a vague idea that Pickles, somehow, never left the place. At least, he was always there. He wondered if Pickles had seen a ball game any more recently than that taxi driver he'd had yesterday.

He looked around the big, clean dressing room with the softly whirring electric fans overhead, the freshly painted lockers, and the freshly plastered walls. He glanced at all the big mysterious machines designed to cure ballplayers' aches and pains—things he'd never suffered from. Pete had explained them to him once, but they didn't register with him because he had had no real contact with them. Names like whirlpool bath and electric diathermy were a couple of them. He forgot the rest. But the dressing room, like the team, was big league by the look alone. He started to remember some of the shoddy dressing rooms he had known in the past and he knew it would not be easy to return to them. Not after a taste of this.

When the team began to troop in, some of them nodded in passing but nobody said anything. It was cool, real cool, that way. They knew by now that Pete had told him how they had voted and so the thing was closed. It had to be. He couldn't see any manager, or front office GM, keeping a ballplayer around when the rest of the team didn't want him. And he knew, without being told, that any other big-league team would be very doubtful about taking him on when they knew why he was sent back down.

He looked over the mail in the box without much expectation. He seldom received any. But this time, in his slot, he saw a letter. It was from Doug, his brother. The return address had "Corp." before his name, so Doug had been promoted. It had been

sent from some town, whose name he couldn't pro-
nounce, in Germany. He opened it and read:

Kid—I got a copy of an old *Sporting News* and I
know you've got it made. It isn't any surprise to me.
You wound up with the team I always dreamed of
playing for. What a break! Don't blow this one,
Danny! And I know you won't. Just give it everything. I've been bragging all over the barracks about
my kid brother and I've got them half believing what
I tell them, that the Blue Sox won the pennant when
they opened the season with you in right field. As
for me, things are going along. . . .

He read it over three times, glad at last, for something. Doug told him about the promotion, said
he'd quit being bitter about his failure to make the
big leagues, and had quit the drinking. Doug was
going great, you could tell from the tone of the letter. You could also tell that he was not envious, but
was getting wonderful kicks that his kid brother had
done what he had failed to do. Danny suddenly
envied Doug, for whom he had always felt sorry.

He put the letter carefully in a pocket of his
jacket, took his glove, and went on up to the field
with the early ones—the utility men. There had

been no sign of Jug Slavin when he'd left. He had the idea that when Jug arrived he would get the word to go see him.

But the word didn't come, and when finally he saw Jug, in the dugout during batting practice, Jug merely said, "The GM was out of town on a quick trip. He'll be back tonight. He'll probably want to talk to you in the morning."

Danny nodded. He should have felt good about the reprieve of a day but he didn't. Rather, he wished to get everything over with—including the inevitable walking papers to Rapid City or wherever.

In his cuts at the plate during batting practice he stung balls to every sector of the park. When he wasn't batting, he was shagging flies or playing at the shortstop position. Berry, the Clipper catcher who kept calling him Rizzuto, couldn't know it, but for years he had played the shortstop position during batting practice. The reason was that he had been advised long ago by some forgotten coach that it would improve his handling of ground balls in the outfield. It was a fact, as he'd found out. Through such practice he had learned to nab those unpredictable hops with the sureness of a shortstop.

He had kept his activity at such a furious pace

that he was sweating when he came into the dugout. He expected no friendly look or gesture today. He didn't get any. But Jug Slavin grudgingly said to him, "You might have been a shortstop. In a pinch you probably could be one."

Danny wanted to get things in the open. He said, "I know about the player vote."

Jug suddenly looked angry. "Players don't run ball clubs. Managers and general managers do. Players are paid to play ball."

It was a straw to grasp at. He could see that Jug was angry because the ballplayers had tried to go over the head of the manager and the front office.

"Better go change that sweat shirt," Jug said.

Danny went to change it. He hoped that Stan Davis, the general manager, felt the same way about the player vote that Jug obviously did.

With a fresh sweat shirt he headed back through the tunnel to the field. He met Rip Radjecki midway. "One more word, Danny," Radjecki said.

Danny waited.

"If they send you down, don't think you're through. I saw the talent, the possible greatness, in you long ago, and on a night when the crowd thought you were lousy. I still see that possible greatness—if something ever wakes you up." Then Radjecki brushed past him and headed to the dressing room.

Danny went to the dugout and found a far corner empty. The line-up for today's game had Duke Page in right field even though a right-hander—Muddy Grand—was going for the Redskins. Danny guessed that Fiske's anemic batting average of the moment, .228, had something to do with that. He glanced down the dugout bench at Fiske and knew he was looking at the face of a ballplayer who would never fade out gracefully. The facts would have to prove it, the slow and hard way, to Fiske.

The crowd wasn't capacity by any means, but it was a large one. Perhaps many had come to hoot the Sox about yesterday's third-base fiasco. Both the Sox and the Redskins had a chance to go into first place—by percentage points—today. The slumping Robins were idle; the Sox and Redskins were tied. This pennant hassle was beginning to look as though any one of five different teams could make it, with one sustained winning streak somewhere along the steamy July-August days when the veterans begin to wilt and the rookies find second wind.

As the game started, Rip Radjecki's parting words

were still tripping through Danny's mind. *If something ever wakes you up.*

If he found the answer, it would no doubt be in Rapid City.

Chapter 21

SEMPLE, THE REDSKIN THIRD BASEMAN, LED OFF WITH a walk, and Lasky looked so annoyed with himself, scuffing the dirt, that Gibbs walked out to talk to him. Apramante, the second hitter, caromed a neat bunt down the third-base line. There was no play possible at second. Scalzi nailed Apramante at first but not by much.

Harley Keene, the right fielder, was a real percentage hitter, who had won the batting championship one year. Lasky worked hard on him, giving him nothing good. Keene refused to swing until the count had run out. Then he fouled two. But Lasky still had the nerve to throw a sharp-breaking curve in that spot and Keene tipped it into Gibbs' big mitt for the second out.

Perhaps it was the intense labor he had put in on

[164]

Keene that caused Lasky to make his first pitch to
Francano, who followed, too good. Francano went
for it greedily and laced it on a sharp line over
Walker's head. Duke Page came racing in, grabbing
the perfect hop in a nice position for a throw.
Danny hadn't expected Semple to try to score, because the ball had not been hit that deep. But Semple never hesitated as he made the turn at third. The
Redskins, Danny decided, were gambling on rookie
nervousness on the throw.

As if to prove they were right, Page did the one
thing that gave Semple a chance. In his eagerness,
probably to show that he had a strong arm, he threw
it all the way to Gibbs on a line. Even though he
didn't overthrow, it didn't help Gibbs the way a
skimming, one-hop peg would have. It arrived in
a curving loop that lost at least a part of a second,
and it was at Gibbs' shoulders. He had to swoop
down with it, instead of having it already down
there on the bounce. The difference was enough
for Semple. He was in, swirling dust, and Gibbs
didn't even argue.

I would have had Semple cold and dead on that
one, Danny thought to himself. He guessed that

Gibbs and Slavin and a lot of other people might be thinking the same thing.

Lasky forced big Vic Powder, the first baseman, to fly harmlessly to Jaffe for the third out.

When the Sox hustled in, Danny saw Slavin talking to Duke Page. Page kept nodding, hard. Danny could guess that Jug was pointing out the mistake he'd made on the throw. Page must have learned better somewhere along the line, but nervousness or something had made him play it the sugarbush way.

When Walker stepped in, the bench jockeys went into action.

"Double play at third!"

"Hey, Alphonse—where's Gaston today?"

"Brooklyn never lived it down—neither will you!"

Walker turned to glare. The fact that it hadn't been his fault didn't make any difference; he had taken part in the now famous Third Base Summit Conference, as one reporter had called it.

Walker took a strike and then swung at a second pitch which looked wide to Danny. Walker wasn't really a lead-off man, never had been. He pushed a weak ground ball to second, which Apramante gobbled up for the first out.

Stookey, batting second with Page in the line-up,

belted one far and high—but too high—to center
field. Purcell was there and waiting for it impa-
tiently as it came down, like a commuter held up
by a late train. In fact, Purcell did everything but
glance at his watch to kill time as it descended.

Woodward advanced to the box and the bench
jockeys went to work again.

"The doubles hitter!"

"Who's on third?"

"You guys don't need a coach, you need a traffic
cop!"

Woodward scuffed dirt backward, in the general
direction of the Redskin bench as his only retort.
Muddy Grand threw him two balls, then he hit the
third pitch for a single to center.

Jaffe stepped in, but they left him alone since he
had not taken part in the third-base mess. Danny
felt the sting of the bench-jockey jeers even though
he wasn't out there to absorb any of them. He knew
that they all knew Walker and Woodward had not
been to blame. He could imagine what a target they
would make of him if he were in this game.

Jaffe put the perfect silencer on the Redskin
bench's rough riders. He caught a Grand curve that
didn't break enough and he rode it through a strong

breeze blowing in, over the high wall and the net on top of the high wall and out of sight. As he followed Woodward across the plate and received the usual hand shake, both of them turned toward the Redskin bench and, in unison, doffed their caps before trotting into the Sox bench.

Scalzi walked and Gibbs was safe on an error by Semple. Duke Page stepped in. It had the makings of one of those big innings that sometimes start, as this one had, with the first two men going out.

Page had a swarthy, muscled look and he took a toe hold in the box. Grand brushed him back with a high hard one and Page took a few steps toward the mound. Grand promptly replied with a few steps toward Page. They exchanged words until Ramono went out and stood between them, while the plate umpire talked to Page.

Grand came in with a knee-high curve that Page took for a strike. The third pitch was wide for a ball. Page hit the next one off the end of his bat and it went plunk-plunk-plunk toward a region just to the right of Powder, on first. Powder reached it and threw to Grand, running hard for the first-base bag. He got there at the approximate time Page did, because the roller had been slow. Page barreled into

Grand, knocking him to the ground and knocking the ball loose from his glove. The umpire spread his hands for the safe sign as Grand got up, furious.

He charged straight at Page, as soon as he saw by a backward glance that Powder had the ball, holding Scalzi at third. Grand took the first swing and Page took the second. Grand's only glanced off Page's outthrust arm, but Page's connected. Grand went down for the second time within seconds, and this time when he arose both benches were emptied.

It took nearly ten minutes for peace to be restored, and it was restored only after the umpire had sent both Grand and Page to their respective dressing rooms. They left, still shouting at each other, and the first Blue Sox rhubarb of the season was over. But the game wasn't, not by eight and a third innings, and if two teams had ever been in the mood to clobber one another, these two were.

With the bases filled now, and the same two outs, the Redskins had hastily warmed up Gary Beall, usually a starting pitcher and just about their best. They wanted this game; that was clear when they brought in Beall.

Beall, still slightly cold, threw three straight balls. But then he hung in with a fast ball that Andy Pearson took. He threw it again and Pearson swung, but the speed overpowered him and the ball turned into a lazy foul into the stands behind first base.

Once more Beall came in with the same straight fast ball. Pearson caught it this time and drove it to center—Purcell's territory and no place for a fluky hit. Purcell gathered it in on the dead run toward the left-field wall and the long, frantic inning was over.

Danny didn't dare look toward Jug as he waited. Somebody had to replace Page. "Somebody" just about had to be Danny Redd, hitting a gaudy .334 or Chip Fiske hitting a dismal .228.

Danny heard Jug's voice from far down the bench. His head came up like a bird dog's on the hunt.

"Take over out there, Chip," Jug called to Fiske.

So that did it. There went his last chance to get back into the line-up before the Slavin-Davis hour of decision in the powwow tonight. Rapid City, here I come, he thought.

Chapter 22

It turned into one of those games that usually take place only deep in September when the pennant hangs on every pitch. The fact that the winner would move into temporary possession of first place was far from the whole reason; it was too early in the season for a series to be that crucial. But the Sox were sick of the endless riding from the bench about yesterday's tragedy at third base; the Redskins were angry because Page had hit Grand and knocked him down, while Grand's punch had missed. It looked like a game where explosions could occur at any moment. All sorts of explosions.

Lasky threw one hard and close to Hold, the long-ball-hitting shortstop, and there was a fast exchange of words between pitcher and batter. Purcell, always an unpredictably fiery competitor, crashed into

[171]

Walker as he broke up a double play. They had to be separated by the nearest umpire.

Gary Beall found his control. Lasky already had his. The innings began to roll along and nothing changed on the scoreboard. By the top of the seventh it was still a 2 to 1 ball game, but nobody in the park thought it would stay that way.

It didn't.

With one out, Keene tripled to left center and Francano promptly brought him across with the tying run on a looper to left. Powder popped to the infield, but Purcell doubled to the corner in left. Then Lasky purposely passed the belter, Hold, to pitch to Ramono.

For the first time in the afternoon Danny saw some baseballs streaming back and forth in the Sox bull pen. Lasky was finally beginning to show a tendency to fade a little in the late innings. It is one of nature's laws about ballplayers whose arms are not made of elastic, but only seem that way for a certain number of years.

Ramono could power a long ball, too, though not with the frequency of Hold. He hit left-handed, held the bat almost at the nub. Lasky had two balls and a strike on him when Ramono crossed up the entire Sox infield. He plunked a bunt down the third-base line that was as perfect as it was unexpected. Neither Lasky nor Scalzi had a chance and the tie-breaking run came in. After that, Lasky struck out Beall but the damage had been done.

The crowd carried the seventh inning stretch into extra minutes, imploring the Sox to get that tying run in fast. Scalzi, leading off, tried mightily. He ripped a line drive low, toward left. But Semple dove and came up with it. The crowd's roar turned into a drawn-out groan.

Gibbs punched at an outside pitch, obviously trying to slap it into right field. But it didn't go high enough and Apramante's late leap took it in.

Fiske advanced from the on-deck circle toward the box. Danny held his breath, wildly hoping against hope that Jug would call Fiske back, send him in to bat for his rival with the .228 average. But Jug didn't do it.

Fiske looked at a ball, then took a strike. He took another ball, then was fooled completely by a change-up. Two and two. Beall came in with a strike and Fiske swung. But he hit under the ball.

It looped into shallow left, near the foul line. Francano was there in plenty of time. Fiske kept running as the ball came down, Francano planted and waiting. And then one of those strange tricks that the sun can sometimes play on an outfielder was played on Francano.

The ball hit his glove, popped out. He dove for it. Too late. It hit the ground, and by the time Francano recovered it Fiske was on second base.

Promptly Fiske called time and started to walk toward the first-base foul line, beckoning to the Sox dugout. Jug went out. They talked. And finally Fiske trudged in, beside Jug. Jug pointed while he called, "Redd!"

Danny walked out in disbelief. As Fiske passed him, Jug stopped. "Chip thinks, and I agree, that there's a better chance of you getting that tying run home on a single than of him getting it in. You're running for him."

Danny turned and raced out. Fiske had actually pulled himself out of the ball game! It was hard to believe, but it was so. A guy who could do that to himself must want to win a ball game worse than Danny could ever remember wanting to win one.

He took a big lead off second. Beall chased him back to the bag once. Then he threw to Pearson.

And Pearson punched the first pitch into right field for a clean single.

It wasn't deep. Not too many runners would have tried to score on it. But Danny had had the jump from the bag and he wasn't surprised to see Madigan wave him in. He slid into the plate easily, two steps ahead of the throw. But he knew, as he arose, that Fiske's decision had meant the run. Fiske would never have brought it in.

When Lasky followed with an infield pop-up, the importance in the switch of base runners was doubly obvious. The run would never have come in. Never.

Chapter 23

WHEN DANNY WENT OUT TO RIGHT FIELD IN THE TOP of the eighth he was ready, in his mind, for the reaction he received. He knew that the fact he had scored the tying run wasn't going to help. The fans counted it as Fiske's run, even though Fiske could never have brought it in.

First he heard a low rumble of voices that turned into one swelling, concerted growl. Then the self-appointed spokesmen who were always present went into action.

"Don't get off the dime, Speed Boy!"

"Take good care of yourself, Brittle Bones!"

"Redd's back—good-by ball game!"

He shut his ears to it. He caught a routine fly on the first Redskin hitter and the bunch in the bleachers roared sarcastic applause, as though he'd made a spectacular save. Getting that important run back seemed to have given Lasky new life and energy. He struck out Semple, and Apramante closed out the top of the eighth by popping to Scalzi near the mound.

But the Sox went down just as meekly. Both teams repeated the act in the ninth. As the game moved into the tenth it was obvious that this game meant much more to both teams than the percentage climb into first place. Every man on the field would find the loss of this one rankling in his mind for weeks to come. These were angry, fired-up pros on both sides; their relentless intensity went far beyond the hoarse enthusiasm of the college yell. Once you nicked the pride of a big-leaguer, you found you had a tiger by the tail.

Nine full innings of pitching a game where every throw had to be decisive finally seemed to have caught up with Lasky. Keene led off with a blow that caromed off the left-field wall. A fast recovery by Woodward held it to a double. But when Lasky followed by losing Francano on the three-two pitch, Jug Slavin emerged from the dugout and waved his left hand toward the bull pen, en route to the mound.

Sam Sloat was the only left-hander warming up. That meant Jug wasn't trusting a regular relief man with this game; he was replacing his Number One starter with his Number Two starter.

The decision pleased the fans, because of Sloat's reputation built up since he had lost his fast ball. The official statistician of the Sox, known as the Brain, had discovered from the elaborate records he compiled that while enemy hitters often got on base against Sloat, they had a very hard time bringing those runners across the plate. Sloat could be free with hits, yet miserly with runs.

Jug and Gibbs and Scalzi kept talking to Lasky while Sloat made the long, slow march in. Lasky looked dejected as he left the mound, despite the tenacious game he had pitched. The crowd roared its admiration to him as he disappeared into the tunnel.

Sloat took the limit of his warm-up throws, conferred for a second time with Gibbs, and then faced big Powder. He threw two balls, two strikes. When Powder hit the fifth pitch, it went just where Sloat had intended it to go.

The swift skim of the ball across the infield skin took it directly to Andy Pearson on a big hop. He shoveled it to Walker. Walker dodged the sliding Francano, leaped, and snapped the ball to Stookey for the double play. That left Keene on third with two outs. A moment later Purcell flied deep to Jaffe in left and the Sox were out of the inning. Sloat trudged in to a tremendous ovation.

Beall hadn't tired. He looked stronger, if anything. He set the Sox down in order. Then the marathon really started. From the tenth through the fourteenth, the only runners who got on base never reached second. The deadly monotonous perfection of Sloat and Beall brought a gradual hush to the crowd. They sensed that some single bit of action would settle this bitter one so swiftly that if the eye moved from the diamond for one long moment, the climax could be missed.

In the bottom of the fifteenth the breakthrough seemed to have arrived at last. Scalzi grounded out. But Pete Gibbs caught a Beall fast ball with the full wood, and for a brief moment it looked like the ball game, then and there.

The line drive streaked to deepest left center, too high for even Purcell to reach. It made an echoing thud off the very top of the wall, ricocheted toward center with Purcell in jackrabbit pursuit. With

Danny, he knew, that ball would have been an in-side-the-park home run; with Gibbs it turned out to be a triple.

Now the Redskins held a conference at the mound and finally Beall got set to face Danny. The infield played him medium deep. He knew that they knew they were in trouble. They had to guard against his patented line-drive singles, and they also had to guard against his speed in beating out a ground ball.

He took a wide one for a ball, then looked down at Madigan for the hit-or-take sign. The sign he got jolted him. Madigan had given him that rarest of all rare signs: the suicide squeeze. Gibbs would be off with the pitch and it was up to Danny Redd to see that his bat met that ball, wherever it came in, to protect Gibbs carrying home the run that would mean the ball game.

He saw why it was a perfect setup for the suicide squeeze. Gibbs was a slow man and the Redskins would not suspect him of daring to come in; Danny was the type of hitter they could not play close, and he could bunt well. Whether he made it to first or not didn't matter. All that mattered was for Gibbs to get across that plate.

Danny got set. He prayed for a low ball. Beall went into the quick stretch and threw.

The pitch couldn't have been worse for the suicide squeeze. It came in faster than any ball Danny had seen Beall pitch, and it came toward his head. He heard the surprised scream of the crowd watching the incredible sight of Pete Gibbs pounding toward the plate without a faltering step.

Now the Sox were committed. It was up to Danny. Either the game ended right here, or else Gibbs was dead and the game could run for another fifteen innings.

His first instinct was to guard his head. He didn't trust those protective helmets the way some ballplayers did. He fell back. Too late he realized that in falling back, in thinking about guarding himself, he had lost the chance to protect Pete Gibbs.

He was sprawled in the dirt, on his back, as he saw that Gibbs had no possible chance. Ramono, all two hundred pounds of him, was waiting for Gibbs with the grim solidity of a concrete wall. Gibbs was a hopeless, abject, pathetically simple out.

But Gibbs refused to accept the fact. He was too

slow to turn around and try to make a dash back and create a rundown situation. There was nothing for Gibbs to do but give up—or crash into Ramono and try to dislodge the ball from his hand.

Gibbs crashed. Both Gibbs and Ramono spun like tops and toppled. But Ramono, the heavier one, held onto the ball. He got up, showing it. Gibbs did not get up. Danny saw him try to, saw him writhe in pain as the umpire's thumb jerked high in the air to signal the out.

Back on his feet, Danny rushed to Gibbs. But by this time half the Sox bench had rushed to Gibbs. Jake Brennan, the trainer, was signaling for a stretcher. Gibbs would have none of it. Three players had helped him to his feet and now he had his arms around the shoulders of two of them.

Suddenly he saw Danny standing there, staring at him. "Danny," he said, "you never even tried to bunt that ball. You took a dive instead."

The look in Pete's eyes was one Danny didn't think he would forget very soon.

Chapter 24

WHEN GIBBS HAD GONE AND THE GAME RESUMED, Danny stepped back into the box. The boos from the stands were so loud he could barely hear Ramono jeering at him. But he heard.

"Thanks for the helping hand, old buddy," Ramono was saying. "Believe me, next time you come back to this league—if you do—I'll see that the Welcome Wagon calls on you."

Danny didn't reply. He couldn't. There were two balls and no strikes on him now, and he stood there watching a fast one cut across the plate, belt high. He was in a daze.

He wasn't thinking so much about how the game could be over by now with the Sox in first place. He was thinking about something he knew was even more important: he'd wrecked the one good friend-

[183]

ship he had, with Pete Gibbs. Pete, who had gone out on the limb for him in every way, was probably headed for the hospital, because Danny Redd had protected himself. Again. Over and over and over, Danny Redd always thought about Danny Redd.

Now finally—too late—he knew what Pete Gibbs and Jug Slavin and Rip Radjecki had been trying to tell him. Radjecki had been trying to tell him this since his first game with the Cortland Colonials. He saw now, as the team and those fans in the stands saw, that though he wore a big-league uniform he was not a big-leaguer.

He watched another strike go by, still wrapped up in his own thoughts. He was a sitting duck for Beall and Beall knew it. So did Ramono.

"Better dodge this next one, China doll," Ramono said.

Danny saw it coming and he lashed at it. He met only air and turned away, hearing Ramono laugh and the crowd roar pure disgust.

He thought, as he trudged toward right field and the cold reception that he knew awaited him, if I only had some of the time I've wasted. But he didn't have time any more. Time had run out on him. He thought again of that look in Pete Gibbs' eyes as they had helped him off the field.

In the top of the sixteenth the Redskins finally made their move. Apramante led off. He touched Sloat for a ground-ball single through the hole between third and short. Keene bunted toward third. Scalzi's usually reliable throw was high. Stookey had to leap. Keene was in by the time Stookey's foot came down on the bag. Redskins were on second and first now, with nobody out. But nobody bothered Sloat. Everyone knew how tough he was when these situations sprang up out of nowhere.

Francano slugged a shot down at Pearson and it almost tied him up in the final knot. He got a glove on it, but it was too swift to stick. He picked it up and threw to Walker in time for the force, but the double play it might have been was far gone by then. Officially, though, it was not an error.

Now Powder became the object of Sloat's attention. One out, men on first and third. Powder didn't wait. He swung at the first pitch and lived to regret it. It was a slider, that fine nickle curve of Sloat's, and it went sky high into the air behind Scalzi.

Scalzi took that one like a trout handling a small floating bug.

Purcell moved in. No one took him lightly. He showed flashes of temper and tantrums now and then, but he was in the slit-your-throat school of ballplayers when a hit meant a ball game. He took a ball. He took a strike. Then he swung and he connected.

It looked, at first, like Woodward's ball as it headed toward right center on the rising line. It really was, too, as Danny saw while racing toward it. But suddenly he saw Woodward stumble slightly, lose his stride. He heard Woodward yell, "Get it, Danny! *Get it!*"

By no rights was it Danny's ball. Anyone could see that. But something had happened to Woodward, and he was out of it. The ball seemed to be resisting the pull of gravity as it continued its relentless rising flight.

There was no time left to watch for warning tracks, for retaining walls, or for converging outfielders. There was no instant left to take the eye off that ball. Danny didn't. He tore the turf under him as he saw Purcell's drive finally start to descend. He reached a point where the ball finally looked

reachable with a last-minute leap. He went into the
air, glove outstretched. He felt the ball sink into
the tightness of the quickly squeezed pocket, and
then he felt the solid impact of a Mack truck, or
whatever it was, run right into the middle of his
back.

Before the sky lost the blue color, he squeezed
more tightly onto the ball in the pocket of the glove.
After that he didn't know a thing. But before he
didn't know a thing he knew he had hold of that ball
for keeps.

Chapter 25

THERE WERE QUITE A FEW PEOPLE AROUND HIM WHEN
he came out of the blank period and most of them
seemed to be ballplayers. The ones in street clothes,
the civilians, he guessed were reporters. The place
he was in looked for all the world like the Sox dressing room and not a hospital. Upon second glance
he saw that it really was. He couldn't be in such
bad shape in that case.

Jug Slavin was coming out of the office and two
men followed him. The two men were Doc Dougherty and the trainer, Jake Brennan. There was an
air of festivity about the big room, although he did
not see any confetti or anything.

Jug chased the players and the reporters away.
Then he leaned over Danny, who had discovered

by this time that he was lying on a cot. Jug said, "How you feeling, Danny?"

"O.K., I think. Did I hold that ball?"

"Like a vise," Jug said. "Look, the Doc here stuck a couple needles in you, so things are probably on the blurred side. You're all right. The Doc is sure."

"But how's Pete?" Danny asked.

"He's so good he's at the hotel. Just shook, that's all."

"That's where I want to go," Danny said. "I want to tell him something."

"You can save it," Jug said. "There's an ambulance outside right now. You're a little more shook than Pete. But don't think anything of it. Just some observation. You'll be out in a couple of days."

Danny nodded again and said, "What happened in the bottom of the sixteenth?"

"Woodward, pulled muscle and all, hit one so far I think it's still in orbit. So we win it. We're in first place and the miserable Redskins are sick, sick, sick."

"Good for them," Danny said.

"Last word, Danny. I think you're over the hump. So does the GM. He got here in time for the last few innings. He says, and I say, once you come out of the hospital and get on your feet, you've got right field wrapped up. All yours."

"I accept," Danny said.

As the men in white were carrying him out on the stretcher, Rip Radjecki slowed them down with a hand wave. He took a long, slow look at Danny and started to grin. "You know, punk," he said, "I'm beginning to think you've got the makings of as big a fool as I used to be."

Danny smiled weakly. Somehow, he thought, it sounded like the highest compliment anyone had ever paid him.